THE MEN I LET DEFINE LOVE

Janelle M Williams

Pen & Pad Publishing LLC

The Men I Let Define Love
Copyright © 2013 by Janelle M. Williams

All rights reserved. Except as permitted under the U.S. Copyright Act of 1976, no part of this book may be reproduced, distributed, or transmitted in any form or by any means, or stored in a database or retrieval system, without the prior written permission of the publisher.

This book is a work of fiction. Names, characters, places, and incidents are the product of the author's imagination or are used fictitiously. Any resemblance to actual events, locales, or persons, living or dead, is coincidental.

Cover design by Steve Jackson. Author photograph by Christopher Barclay.

Printed in the United States of America

ISBN 978-0-9833134-5-8

Pen & Pad Publishing LLC
PO Box 34233
Washington, DC 20043

http://www.penpadpublishing.com
http://www.twitter.com/penpadpublish
jasmin@penpadpublishing.com

Publisher's Cataloging-in-Publication Data

Williams, Janelle M.
 The men I let define love / Janelle M. Williams.
  p. cm.
 ISBN: 978-0-9833134-5-8 (pbk.)
 ISBN: 978-0-9833134-6-5 (e-book)
 1. Man-woman relationships—Fiction. 2. Self-realization in women—Fiction. 3. Dating (Social customs)—Fiction. 4. African American college students—Fiction. I. Title.
PS3623.I55678 M45 2013
813—dc23
                                                             2013931529

To the man who taught me to love and,
just as importantly, passed on his love
for literature – my father,
Michael Fredrick Williams

Dear Readers,

For two years, I let *The Men I Let Define Love* write itself. Yes, it took two years and change to write a 150-page book. Every detail, every word had to be justifiable. I couldn't see anything but the page in front of me, and it took over my life. It took over my lunch breaks, my nightly dreams and my conversations. At times, I hated my protagonist because she was always around.

The fun part lay in writing from the heart. I got a chance to merge real life experiences with pure fiction. I had the opportunity to transcribe the story that I've always wanted to read. And at some point my main character, Kelly Brown, became one of my best friends.

I was lucky enough to stumble upon Pen & Pad Publishing LLC, an independent publishing company, as I neared the completion of my book. I began doing some work for the company and things fell into place from there. But I must stress that I don't think it was my destiny to publish with Pen & Pad; it was the story's destiny. What the story wants and needs is what the story should get.

A writer's work is lonely, and if you plan on taking the independent route, it's unbelievably lonelier. Scary too. There's no big publishing deal to remind you that you're an amazing writer, that there's an audience awaiting you, or that you'll make money. But there is the hope that you'll write a book that's unapologetically honest and fashionably raw. That was, and still is, my dream for *The Men I Let Define Love*.

Now that it's ready for all of you to read, I have grown confident. I am not so certain that it will be a New York Times bestseller or that it will become a major motion picture, but my confidence lies in the fact that I have done the story justice.

For an independent writer, you can equivocate the marketing phase to being in the jungle. Broadcasting a book to the masses is hardly a one-person job. Thankfully, I have great friends who are helping me pick up the slack.

I hope *The Men I Let Define Love* leaves you with a little more love than you started with. I hope you find it as witty and charming as I intended it to be. I hope you request a sequel.

Happy Reading,

Janelle M

CHAPTER ONE:
THE INNOCENT ONE

If love was an algebraic equation,
somewhere I'd miscalculated.

I had less than four months to find him, whoever *he* was. Growing up, I pitied the women who went to college with the goal of securing a husband, so I'm not quite sure when I became one of them. It was probably sometime around my first visit to the historically black college Davis University for a campus tour over spring break my senior year of high school. That spring break I was introduced to the Davis man, and I've been addicted ever since. Addicted to the point where you might find me barefoot in traffic like Edie Sedgwick or singing the blues like Billie Holiday.

HBCU men are smooth, tailored and intelligent. They're Andrew Young, Stokely Carmichael and Thurgood Marshall. I just knew I'd find a Davis University husband to have future Davis University babies with. But all I'd found so far were the butts and ends of love. I kept my eyes peeled and considered my African American studies professor. His tight skin made him look much younger than he was. Though he was bald, the half-inch of hair on his chin shone much more salt than pepper.

Why did I wait until my last semester to take this class, I wondered, transfixed in my usual seat in the very back of his classroom. This particular seat allowed me to intensely stare at the man before me without risk of others noticing my ogling, or so I hoped. I gazed at this man as he spoke, seduced by his genius.

I knew that unlike these twenty-year-old kids that I'd lost time to, he wouldn't disapprove of my dark skin or shapeless body. It would be all about our minds with him. Dismissing our thirty-eight-year age gap, I became completely attentive as he mediated a class debate on the use of the n-word.

"I was raised in a mixed neighborhood. My best friends are black, white, Hispanic... They all use the n-word, and I'm not offended," argued a girl a few rows in front of me. Her confession made me roll my eyes. "I hadn't even experienced racism until this past year," she continued.

I gasped in horror of her naivety. We experience racism every day as it's embedded in the structure of our society. I wanted to yell at her, but I kept quiet. Thankfully, the professor seemed to agree with my silent protest, which made me love him all the more.

"That was your first time experiencing it interpersonally," he said. "But surely you have a friend or a family member who's in a different place than you because of the disparities in our education and judicial system." His sentiment made me quiver, just as his previous lectures had.

I noticed the time, one o'clock on the nose. The professor hadn't stopped speaking, but class was over. I quickly gathered my books and rushed to the door. One o'clock meant that if I didn't make it out of Fontenot Hall in approximately five minutes, I would run the risk of bumping into my last disappointment.

I charged my way through the incoming crowd, stealing a glance at my friend Greg.

"Kelly," he called.

"Sorry. Gotta go. Next time," I shouted back at him without stopping.

I walked quickly. Actually, I almost ran through the long outdated hallway, which had been painted one too many times. I sighed with relief as I hit the double doors. The sun hit my face, and I took in the shivering winds of January. I let them blow through my long black hair. I wanted to do jumping jacks or a dance of some sort. But I opted to save that for the confinement of my room. Instead, I took pleasure in adding one more day to the count. Today marked the 25th day I hadn't spoken to Duane.

I rounded the corner and headed down Columbia Avenue. This particular street in Doberville, Maryland, was always filled with blue-collar workers, rowdy neighborhood kids, a few junkies and the college students who bobbed and weaved through it all. I tried not to wince as I spotted Duane's silver hatchback. He loved that car. I had the urge to key it. I paused, remembering the last conversation we had in that car.

"There are only four options," I said, purposely choosing to leave out my ideal solution in the hopes that he would bring it up himself. "We can be friends, just friends. We can completely call it quits. Or things can go on the way they are... Only, I don't think I can go on like this."

"Why not?" he interjected. "I like the way things are." His elegance was natural. Even when I was threatening to end our makeshift relationship, he was slow and steady, choosing his words with caution and charisma. "We've only been talking for three months now. I don't want to rush things."

But there lie the problem. We were still just *talking* – dating without the title – after three months.

"I just don't feel like we're headed in the right direction. But, I never gave you the fourth option."

"Let's hear it," he said.

"We can continue to talk but talk to other people as well." It was most guys' dream to have their cake and eat it too. But Duane shook his head, a clear no.

"I know myself. I can't talk to you *and* talk to other girls. That's just not me." I could tell that he was being honest. "And, I can't sit back and watch you talk to other guys."

"Well, I can't do this. I won't. I won't be one of those girls. If you really like me and you really care, be *with* me!" There was that option I'd left out. I guess I couldn't help myself. I couldn't stand the thought of checking the "it's complicated" box on my Facebook page.

"I just don't want to make the same mistake twice. With my last girlfriend, I was vulnerable. It hurt. I need time to make things different with you," he pleaded.

I considered this. Maybe he was right. But I was scared. Ever since he told me his biggest fear was being alone, I wondered whether or not I was simply a babysitter, temporarily keeping him safe and entertained.

"Maybe you're just afraid to be alone?"

"Maybe. To some extent, that's why everyone chooses to spend time with someone. Maybe we should just be friends," he said casually. His words crushed me as all hope for a relationship plummeted. But I held my composure, refusing to let him see me break down.

Without a goodbye, I opened the passenger door and rushed out. "I hope you don't think I'm some softy now," he chuckled out the window. It must be nice to be able to chuckle when you stop dating the person you were just whispering sweet nothings to the night before. I guess I was just a bit more... affected.

"Kelly!" DJ stood dangling my keys above my head, taunting me with his usual smile and engaging me with questioning eyes. "You dropped these. Are you alright?" He laughed. "You looked like you were about to key Duane's car." I stood motionless, mouth agape.

"I..." It was hard for me to say much of anything. "I wasn't," I finally managed to squeak out. His laughter continued, and I couldn't help but start to laugh with him.

"You're funny," he said through breaths. "Don't do anything you'll end up regretting." He dropped my keys in the bag that hung half open off my shoulder. Without another word, he was gone. And with a sigh and a half-smile, I continued on to my dorm.

I had the *luxury* of living in The Villas, a dormitory that not only housed upperclassmen but the city's mice and roaches as well. I wasn't sure which was worse, the rodents or my suitemate. I hardly used the kitchen because I was always too scared that I'd find a furry friend in a cabinet or my suitemate's spoiled milk in the refrigerator. Knowing that this was waiting for me when I got to my room turned my half-smile into a grimace.

"Perk up," said the lady behind the front desk as she checked my ID to make sure that I was a resident before I could pass to the elevator bank. I forced a smile for her.

I bypassed the elevators and entered the stairwell as I was only on the second floor. When I reached the last suite door down the hall, I opened it slowly, almost expecting the latch to release a pile of mess that would consequently tumble out. It didn't. Still, I decided it best to plug my nose, close my eyes and feel for my bedroom door. I slid the key into the hole, not daring a peek. I kept my eyes shut until I was in my room with the door closed.

"Ahhh," I screamed when I finally opened my eyes and realized I wasn't alone in the room. "Tamika, what are you doing in here? How did you get in?" I yelled after recognizing my best friend.

"Your door was unlocked," she said. "I didn't want anyone walking in on me, so I locked it just now." She was sitting cozily in her lacrosse sweats at my desk, computer open, typing. Her afro was unusually well kept that day, making her head look a bit too large for her petite body. Somehow it all worked for her though – the afro, the sweats, her unassuming air. "Are you mad? Ugh! You know I don't get a good Internet connection in my room," she pleaded.

"I know," I said warily. "Next time, shoot me a text. What are you working on?"

"A story. It's for my internship. It's about a girl who's missing. She's schizophrenic so they have no idea where to even begin looking for her. It's really sad," she said with clear frustration. Tamika was the type of journalist who threw her whole heart into each story. I was sure it was what would make her successful.

"Hmm. Well, I hope they find her. Maybe your story will help."

"Yeah. Maybe," she said, then closed her computer. "So what are we doing tonight? Happy hour?"

Tamika and I spent most Friday nights at Lemon and Salt, a lounge not too far from our dorm with a respectable happy hour. Respectable meaning we didn't have to show our IDs and could always get free drinks. We were regulars.

"I don't know. You know Duane goes there. I don't really feel like running into him," I complained.

I'd met Duane, a transfer student from Utah, at Lemon and Salt a little over five months ago. He was there with DJ – the premier disc jockey at Davis, so premier that he completely dropped his legal name to go by "DJ" – and Matthew, a shoe-in for a Crest commercial with a smile that showed off all 32 of his pearly whites.

DJ and Matthew were inseparable. I was a little surprised to see them with a third leg. But there stood Duane, in between the two, fitting in flawlessly. I wondered if he could be the one. And so it began.

His smooth caramel skin and high cheekbones were adorable. He wasn't the tallest guy, but he held his own. Some guys were good about working with what they got, and Duane was one of them.

He wore denim on denim. A friend once told me that only Jay-Z could get away with that. I begged to differ as Duane pulled it off effortlessly. In his mismatched denim jeans and shirt, he was very confident as he approached me.

As I got to know Duane, I realized that he was more introverted than he appeared that night. And he was also innocent. Like me, he was a virgin. He didn't even know what breasts felt like. The first time he got a hold of one of mine, he asked what it was made of. "Milk," was his guess, which was more scary than sweet.

"So what! He shouldn't stop you from having fun. C'mon! This is the first weekend in how many that I don't have practice?" Tamika begged.

"Well..." I thought out loud.

"Kelly!"

"Yeah, I guess you're right," I said with a smile. "Let's go."

Brianna was the first one ready that night. She was always the first one ready. Tamika and I met her at a house party freshman year. Alongside us, she was the first one there and also the last to leave.

"Keeelllyyyy," sang her all too familiar voice outside of my room a couple of hours later followed by a knock. Bri loved the bar. Or at least she loved boys and booze, both of which she went through all too quickly.

"Hold on. I'm..." Before I could finish my sentence, she opened the door and took a seat in my chair. "No privacy," I muttered.

"Well, can you hurry up? I'm ready to go," she whined.

"Where's Tamika?" I asked.

"Getting ready."

"Then why don't you go bug her?"

"Because you're the reason why we're always late." I rolled my eyes, but I had no grounds to argue. No matter how much money I spent on clothes, I could never find anything to wear. I threw on my favorite pair of jeans, the ones that made my butt look existent and scrounged for a top. Though it was twenty degrees outside, rationalizing that it would be warm in the lounge, I chose to wear my hot pink racer back tank top. I slid it on and searched the room for my riding boots.

"Ready," said Tamika as she appeared in the doorway. She'd pushed back her afro with colorful ribbon and opted for flats instead of heels. As usual, we were on the same page. Brianna had outdone the two of us in her mini dress and heels. Her opaque tights would have their work cut out for them in keeping her warm.

"Darn," I muttered. "Two minutes." I searched my caboodle

for the makeup I hardly ever wore. I wanted to look my best, just in case I ran into someone unexpected... or maybe I was *expecting* to run into Duane. I quickly applied my mascara and blush, and just as quickly, we were out the door.

Once inside Lemon and Salt, Brianna made a bee line for the bar. Tamika and I headed after her. It was only seven o'clock, but the place was packed. We inched through parties of people until we caught up. Brianna was waiting for us with drinks in hand. Even for Brianna, that was record timing.

"This round's on me," she said. It wasn't unlike Brianna to buy us all drinks. She kept a job so she was one of the few college students who kept a steady flow of cash. Additionally, she enjoyed caring for the people who cared for her. "There's Kenny. I'll be back." She skipped off to see the same guy who she'd screamed she couldn't stand the day before.

Tamika and I just laughed until Tamika abruptly froze.

"What?" I asked.

"DJ's here."

"Aww. Did you guys get into a fight?"

DJ and Tamika were an unofficial item, which meant they did everything that couples did but off the record. They were both single and free to date other people, but if either of them actually did, they were sure to fight about it. They were definitely in the "complicated" arena.

"Umm, no." She paused. "Duane's with him." My muscles tightened, then suddenly there was silence. No, the music hadn't stopped, but I'd spotted Duane and he'd created the silence in my mind – and the nausea I was feeling as well.

Duane was still a virgin because he had a saint for an ex-girlfriend. Even though she was miles away in Utah, she intimidated me. Or maybe their past relationship intimidated me. They'd met in church. I imagined them singing together in the choir, reading their bibles instead of going to the movies, and praying instead of making out. I guess I just wanted a piece of that with him. Instead of his spiritual equal, I felt like his jezebel. He hadn't given me the title of girlfriend yet he'd touched my boob.

It was still so hard for me to let go of him. At some point, I honestly began to believe that he was the last good guy left. I simply overlooked the fact that he still hadn't the faintest idea of what he wanted to do with his life. This should have been a red flag. He'd appeared to be a sincerely sweet guy, but the fact that he couldn't commit to me anymore than he could a major naturally bruised my ego.

After our conversation in his car that day, I literally avoided him like the plague. He pleaded, to no avail, for friendship. It was just something that I couldn't offer him. I was done wasting time on the wrong boy, and I was hurt. After twenty-four-and-a-half days, it didn't hurt any less, but I couldn't avoid him any longer.

Before I knew it, DJ and Tamika were headed to the dance floor, leaving Duane and I alone.

"Hey, Kelly Brown," he said formally. He was the definition of awkward.

"Hey. How are you?" I asked.

"I'm alright. You?"

"I'm good. Where's Matthew?"

"At home," he said. "Some type of stomach virus."

"Oh," I said, trying to think of the best way to get out of this conversation without letting on that he had hurt me.

My mind practically leapt with glee when I saw Greg walking toward us. I could spot the surplus of facial hair that surrounded his big lips and the one dimple on his round, caramel face anywhere. Normally, I wouldn't be this happy to see him, but tonight, I was ecstatic over anything that would alleviate this awkward conversation.

"W'sup, Kelly," said Greg coolly, looking around. I had never seen him at Lemon and Salt before. He looked uncomfortable and out of place. He was a brain, by any man's definition. He only looked entirely comfortable with his head in a book or behind his guitar. In turn, he wasn't nearly as sociable as the rest of the students at Davis. Still, he'd found a way into my life freshman year, and we'd been good friends ever since.

"Do you know Duane?" I asked, placing my hand on Duane's shoulder. It was unbearably cold to my touch, as if I had a Mr. Freeze affect on him. What had time done to me? What had time done to us?

"No," he answered. I slowly removed my hand from Duane's shoulder. It, too, had become icy cold – and noticeably shaky.

"Well, this is Duane. Duane, this is Greg," I said. They gave each other a head nod.

For the next couple of minutes, we all just stood there, nodding our heads and swaying to the music. Duane was the one to break the silence.

"See you around, Kelly." With that, he was gone. Had my vision been better, I may have seen the wind that followed him, cold and swift. Was that it? He'd spent weeks trying to be my friend, but when we were placed in a room together, he said nothing. He just walked away.

The night progressed, and I appreciated the constant flow of drinks that kept my mind from obsessing over Duane. We were having a good time. Brianna, the life of the party, pranced around the place, finding friends at every table. Greg was talking to a cute girl whose attention he'd caught. Tamika and I were dancing, two of only a few in the crowd who weren't bumping and grinding.

"It's getting hot. I need a break," I said and headed off the dance floor. Tamika followed.

Since we were both at our drink max, we thought it best to get water. On our way to the bar, we ran into DJ.

"Tamika! Kelly! Where you going?" he asked.

"To the bar. For water. Move, Deej, you're in the way." I playfully nudged him. He laughed, giving me a big bear hug. I hugged him back until I realized that he wouldn't let me move. DJ and I had a tight relationship. He was like an older brother in that he was always looking out for me. I could tell that he was trying to save me from something now. My only guess was that this was about Duane. "DJ, let me go. I'll be fine."

That was a lie. Duane was in the far corner of the bar with a girl. I watched as his lips moved along her neck and his hands to the small of her back. I didn't want to look any longer, but I couldn't move. Eventually he lifted his head, and his eyes met mine. They were unapologetic, providing no excuses. My eyes swelled as I abruptly turned for the door. Just being innocent didn't make him such a good guy after all.

It wouldn't be long before Duane lost his virginity, and it wouldn't be the first time that a good guy got caught up in the Davis ratio. There were four girls for every guy enrolled, and most guys made sure to use that to their advantage. The prettiest, smartest, funniest girls were often left desperate, pleading to guys who should've been begging for their attention. That just wasn't me. I vowed to never desperately plead again. Also, I vowed to never date another transfer virgin.

Tamika and I were silent as we walked back to The Villas. I didn't feel much like talking, and I suspected that she didn't know what to say. So when we reached the dorm, I took the stairs to the second floor and Tamika took the elevator to her room on the eighth.

"I'll call you later," she said as we parted ways.

I crashed into bed with racing thoughts, all filled with memories of Duane. Suddenly, I realized that none of these memories were really... memorable. There *had* to have been good times, I thought to myself. But none came to mind.

I remembered singing in his car, belting out Danity Kane. I loved singing in the car so maybe that was a good moment. But, I don't remember what he added to it. Not a harmony. Not a note. Frankly, I don't even remember him being there. I just remember being in his car.

I remembered introducing him to sushi, spicy tuna rolls to be exact. I'd read that trying something new really brings a couple together. He liked them. But as I remember it, he never repaid the favor. He didn't take the time to introduce me to anything new, not to mention that I currently hate spicy tuna rolls. I got sick after eating them once, and I've yet to regain those taste buds.

I remembered going to the movies with him. The seats had those awkward hand rests, the ones that don't lift. Though we went to see a movie he chose, he fell asleep on my shoulder within the first fifteen minutes. His head was heavier than I thought it would be.

But there had to have been good moments... All I knew was that despite not being able to recall any good times, I was wasting my time thinking about a boy that wasn't thinking about me.

My phone rang, putting an end to those thoughts. When I picked up my phone, I wasn't sure whether I should answer. *Tayo* flashed across the screen.

"What does *he* want?" I wondered out loud. Tayo was a friend of mine, but things always got a little too friendly between the two of us. I didn't know what to expect from him, but I ultimately welcomed his distraction from thoughts of Duane.

"Hello," I answered.

"Hey, Kels," he said. "Got a minute?"

"Hmm. Depends. What's going on?" I asked, trying to sound cheery.

"Nothing. I just wanted to talk to you. It's been a while."

"Yeah, I know. How's the job?"

Tayo was a year older than me. He graduated last spring to become a third grade teacher at a local elementary school. It was a career that suited him well. He was patient and illustrative. I listened to the ups and downs of teaching, waiting for a hint as to why he really called.

"I want to see you," he said. Tayo and I hadn't talked in months because he didn't know how to be a platonic friend to me. Duane had interrupted an interesting relationship between the two of us. We both liked each other a bit more than friends should, but it was hard for Tayo to accept my virginity so we never managed to move things beyond the friend stage. He never pressured me, but somehow I knew it resonated with him. Tayo was the opposite of Duane. He was far from innocent. He was everything but innocent.

"I don't know," I said hesitantly. But I did miss him. He was easy to talk to and very caring. Talking to him about Duane would help. And because Tayo was so rugged and protective, I found it easy to snuggle up to him. I couldn't deny liking the way his big arms held me close.

"I just want to be around you. No gimmicks, no ulterior motives," he said. I considered it.

"Not tonight. Can I call you back tomorrow?"

"Yeah. Sure. Talk to you tomorrow."

After lying in bed for hours, I finally drifted off to sleep.

That Saturday morning I carried out my fantasy and keyed Duane's car. Well, no, I didn't. But I really thought about it. I made it as far as his car again. It was parked outside of The Villas, probably just while he was visiting DJ. Oddly enough, I'm not sure that it was my conscience that stopped me. It was the fact that I knew Duane would just inflict his own damage on the car again anyway, and his parents would pay to fix any scratches I put in it along with whatever new dents he caused. That was the way it worked in the past.

Duane was a very poor driver. We almost got into an accident on our first date. We managed to successfully get in one on our fourth date.

Instead of keying his car, I found myself sending him one final text message. It read, "You're a virgin who can't drive." Thank you, Brittany Murphy. I couldn't help but smile at my *Clueless* reference.

I didn't return Tayo's phone call that weekend. I also didn't receive any calls, texts, BBMs or Facebook messages from Duane. Not even a tweet. Most of me never wanted to talk to him again, but a small part of me wished he would call and apologize, admitting that he'd made a huge mistake on Friday and in letting me go entirely.

When Monday morning came, going to class was the last

thing I wanted to do. But at least I would get to see my professor.
I dressed my best to attend his class, but that was nothing out of the ordinary. Davis students were into fashion. Everyone was making his or her own grand statement. Chic. Afrocentric. Professional. Sexy. Retro. Urban. I was no exception. I considered myself classic and girly. Though I wasn't one to hike to class in heels, I made sure that I was always giving off the right impression... cute, feminine, unique and intelligent. I was confident that my look said all of that at first glance.

I wore my favorite green sweater with a jean skirt, leggings and boots. As I made my way to my first class, I looked good even if I didn't feel it.

I walked into Humanities and couldn't help but be confronted with the ratio. There were nearly forty students in this class – only four were boys. I took a seat by one of the four and half-listened to a discussion on Shakespeare's *Othello*.

I was simply going through the motions as I staggered to Economics, my least favorite class because I didn't get the concepts and I didn't like taking notes on a subject I knew I would never understand. It was always so hard to concentrate, waiting and anticipating my twelve o'clock class with my favorite professor. It never came soon enough.

I waited. And waited. And waited. Until I finally heard, "Well that's it for today, guys. Please remember to read. If you don't read, you will not pass." I hated reading for econ. I reluctantly picked up my barely used book and made my way to the door.

Completely erasing the economic experience, I walked into my favorite class with a smile on my face.

"'Why am I writing this book? Nobody asked me to.' Does anyone recognize that quote?" Class had started, and a few hands shot up. I kept mine down, not able to place the quote.

"Frantz Fanon. *Black Skin, White Masks*," said a girl in the front row of the room.

"Very good," he said. "If you have not read *Black Skin, White Masks* by the time you graduate..." He sighed. "Please find time to read this book." He shook a well-worn book in his left hand.

There was always so much to gain from hearing him speak. He knew so much and yet he spoke as if he honestly believed he could learn more from us students. Each Monday, Wednesday and Friday I was hypnotized by his lecture. Today, I left class in search of a book that I had about four months to read, in addition to finding a man of course.

Instead of dreading Tuesday, where I'd find myself at my internship, pitching reporters and stacking Cokes in the meeting room, at the close of this particular Monday, I found myself forgetting Duane and remembering Tayo. I really *did* miss him. So I dialed his number.

CHAPTER TWO: THE GRADUATE

**Every girl loves a well-fitting pair of jeans.
How unfortunate when they rip.**

He wasn't a graduate when I met him. He was a junior, and I was a sophomore. Even then, I felt like he was much older and wiser. Like I was a little girl in comparison. Much worse, I was the little girl with the black eye. A lacrosse ball had hit me smack in the face at one of Tamika's games.

"Whoa, who fucked you up?" was the first thing he said to me. Then, "I'm sorry. It just looks really bad."

I was mortified as DJ stepped in and formally introduced us. DJ and I were still in the process of developing our close friendship. But even then, I was comfortable telling him that I had a little crush on Tayo. Well, I was comfortable until I realized that DJ wasn't too thrilled with my little crush.

"It wouldn't be a good match. Trust me. Besides, he's dating someone, and they're getting pretty serious."

What he didn't tell me was that Tayo had expressed interest in me too. I wouldn't find that out until over a year later when I spilled the beans to Tayo about the schoolgirl crush I had on him sophomore year. Turns out, DJ had dissuaded the two of us from talking to each other. Often, I wondered why DJ was so keen on keeping the two of us apart. I've come to the conclusion that DJ was either looking out for me or crushing on me. After all, this was before I introduced him to Tamika.

Either way, he was right. That girl seriously became the first love of his life. But a little over a year later, she seriously broke his heart when she cheated on him.

Our friendship grew parallel with their relationship. But, he never cheated on her. Not with me at least. Women's intuition told me not at all. He was one of the few guys who seemed to have a clear understanding of monogamy and respect for commitment.

But what if DJ had played matchmaker? What if that girl hadn't broken Tayo's heart? What if she hadn't been in the picture at all? What if he had met me first? I guess there would still be the issue of sex...

I had religion and fear to thank for my virginity. My Christian upbringing wouldn't let me lose it, and friends' stories didn't help either. When girls lost their virginity, they went crazy – crazy for sex and crazy for the guy who introduced them to it. I hadn't done much of anything. Tayo had done it all.

Tayo and I talked for hours that Monday night. Neither of us dominated the conversation. We took turns telling stories and asking questions to get caught up on each other's lives.

I always knew we'd make a great couple. He was big and edgy; I was petite and conservative. On the inside, he was molten and I was obstinate. As opposites, we complemented each other. I could tell him anything, just as he could tell me. We embraced this comfort, releasing our secrets, embarrassments and fears without judgment.

I listened to Tayo talk about his mother and father. They were Nigerian and strict, to put it lightly. On a teacher's salary, he had moved back into his parents' place to save money. As a consequence, he was now suffering from the "back home" blues. Living under his parents' roof again had put limitations on his lifestyle. No drinking and no girls sleeping over meant no freedom and a pretty dull existence based on Tayo's standards. But the free, home cooked meals every day made the conditions bearable. Yet, with breakfast, lunch *and* dinner, his mom was setting a standard that no girlfriend could live up to.

"Can you believe that she answered my cell phone the other day?" he complained about his mother. Despite his protests, he and I both knew that he was the world's biggest mama's boy.

"Well," I said, "moving out is always an option." I constantly teased Tayo about living with his parents. I never mentioned how much I admired the way he sucked it up to save for graduate school. Most boys frivolously threw away their money on cars, girls and clothes. Fancy a guy who wanted to educate himself.

"Yeah, yeah." He laughed. "Maybe I'll just move in with you."

"There's no one here to clean up behind you so that wouldn't work," I joked. I couldn't fathom what it would be like to live together. What I knew for sure was that we could never manage to stay on steady ground living apart. We'd be on great terms for weeks until something small set one of us off.

"At least I'd get a chance to see you. But I won't beg."

I wanted to see Tayo too. I just didn't want things to end like they had the last time. He'd unexpectedly stalked out of my room months ago, saying something about not being able to be my friend. He thought I was falling for him. Said it scared him shitless – the after-effect of a broken heart. Usually I would have called him the next day to mend the rift, but the next day I met Duane.

"Fine," I said. "This weekend we should meet up."

I hadn't told Tayo that I'd stopped talking to Duane. So I was anxious to hear what he would say on the matter. I just didn't want him to think that I'd dumped Duane for him. That would prove too much for him.

The week passed without much to remember it by. Friday usually meant one thing, Lemon and Salt, but that was now out of the question. I couldn't bear the thought of running into Duane again.

The hurt he'd caused came in pulses. One moment I didn't care, and the next I was angry enough to throw a punch. Little of it had to do with romantic feelings. I wasn't in love with Duane, and a strong part of me knew that I never would be. That same part of me was going mad.

I knew the statistics and the ratios. I knew that I was getting older without the prospects getting any better. I knew that Duane might be the only guy interested in dating a virgin, and his interest proved to be short-lived. On top of all of that, I knew that I was hard to please. Emotions aside, I *was* in love with the thought of Duane.

It was time to get out.

"Tamika!" I screamed, "This is how you treat a friend in need?"

"Kelly, I can't go out with you every night. I've already made plans. I'm sorry," she said, super composed as usual.

"Maybe I'll just call DJ and cancel for you."

"We both know that you wouldn't do that. Call Brianna."

"Fine," I snapped, hanging up to dial Brianna.

"Hey, Kelly," she answered. Her voice was muffled. Wherever she was, it was very loud. There was shouting and laughter in the background.

"Where are you?" I asked. It sounded like she was at a party, but it was only half past five in the afternoon.

"Kyle's house. He's having an all-day soiree. I told you about it weeks ago. You should come over."

"I don't know. I don't really like Kyle. Ever since that night at O'Reily's..." Kyle and I had gotten into an argument not too long ago. He'd playfully called me a bitch, and I not so playfully kicked him in the balls.

"Who cares? Everyone is here. Please come."

"Well, alright, but only because everyone is there. I still don't like Kyle."

"Who does?" Brianna joked.

After walking the three blocks to Kyle's house, I paused at the staircase that led to a poorly maintained porch. I had no idea what I was doing here. Was I *this* desperate for human interaction? But I was already here so I figured I might as well go in, right? I walked the length of the steps and knocked on the door.

"Kellllly," rang Brianna's voice. "You let us start the party without you," she pouted. I could tell that she was well into her third or fourth drink.

"What? I thought I *was* the party." We both laughed while I snuck a look at who else was attending the all-day soiree. I made out the faces of a few friends, a few associates, and to my surprise, a lot of people who I'd never seen before.

"Um, when you said everyone is here, you meant everyone in what sense? I don't know most of these people, and neither do you. Do they even go to Davis?"

"I do know them. There's Jason, Kerry, Ryan, Segun, Ashley, Brittney. Some of them go to Davis, but we have a pretty good representation of the neighborhood here."

I rolled my eyes at her apparent popularity. "How do you know *everyone*?" I asked with a dubious grin. She shrugged her shoulders and led me further into the party, introducing me to more unfamiliar faces.

I wasn't paying too close attention to the new people I was meeting. I was sure that come tomorrow I wouldn't be able to remember a single name. That's probably because I didn't really *care* to remember any of their names. I just didn't want to think about boys like Duane anymore.

"Kevin, my favorite." Brianna motioned to a jock in the middle of the crowded room. He wasn't the center of attention, but it wasn't hard to notice the multiples of eyes that watched him as he made his way through the crowd. Calling him cute would be an understatement. He had a flawlessly symmetric face with a chiseled body that made it obvious he was a football player. He wore a fresh fade and relaxed apparel. His cool manner made me wonder whether or not he was ridiculously cocky or all together oblivious to the attention he was receiving.

"W'sup, Bri," he said, giving her a big hug. "How long have you been here?"

"Pretty much all day," she answered.

"Who's your friend?" he asked.

"I'm Kelly," I answered for her.

"Kevin," he said, holding out his hand.

Some guys liked to let handshakes linger. Those awkward shakes were always a bit too sensual for me. And of course there were the guys who barely shook your hand. That dead fish handshake automatically screamed, "pushover." Finding a guy who could give a proper handshake was almost as complicated as finding one to love, and I was close to giving up on both accounts. But when a guy like Kevin came along, a girl had no choice but to keep hope alive. Thank you, Jesse Jackson. His handshake was as perfect as his appearance.

Two hours and a couple of drinks later, I found myself having fun. Kyle had shared a few impolite words with me, but they hadn't left a mark. I was enjoying this new company. With Davis being such a bubble, it was always nice to experience new people. Plus, with everyone talking and dancing sans sloppy drunks and belligerent dudes, the party was quite pleasant.

Though I'd come to the soiree to get my mind off of guys, Kevin had easily and certainly drawn my attention. He was amiable and handsome. He was funny, but he wasn't the joke of the night either. The only thing that I found bothersome about him was that he didn't seem to be paying anyone, myself included, an unusual amount of attention. He just moved around pools of people, flashing a grin. It seemed as if he was making small grandeur appearances though there was nothing pretentious about him. He could easily be *the one*.

He walked into the kitchen. Taking advantage of my empty cup, I headed in after him. He poured his drink and turned around to see me standing behind him, waiting to do the same.

"How is it?" he asked, indicating the party with his head.

"I like it," I said with a nod. "Nice group, I think." He held his hand out for my empty cup.

"Yeah. I'm glad you're having a good time. You looked a little... uncomfortable when you walked in." He finished pouring my drink and handed me the newly filled cup. I hated to think that I'd looked awkward upon arrival, but I was glad to hear that he'd noticed me. Maybe he was paying me some attention after all.

"It's just... Kyle and I aren't really on the best terms."

He laughed. "He's a goof, whatever he did." He shook his head and shrugged his shoulders. Letting down my guard, I laughed with him. After all, goof was the perfect word to describe Kyle.

"What year are you?" I asked after our laughter subsided.

"I'm a junior," he answered.

How was it possible that I hadn't noticed him? Had boys like Duane and Tayo really blinded me? Kevin definitely wasn't easy to miss. With less than four months until graduation, I needed to be more aware.

"Seg," he called over my head. "Talk to you later, Kelly." He placed a hand on my shoulder and gave it a light squeeze as he made his way through the crowd to a small guy, Segun, who was making some type of a stir back in the party room.

Satisfied with the short exchange but still aching for his number, I made my way back into the mix in search of Brianna. I found her joking and laughing in the center of a small group of people. I maneuvered my way into the group and began to laugh with them, even throwing out a few jokes of my own from time to time.

It wasn't long before I left the soiree, without another word to Kevin. Maybe he was the type to admire from afar. Maybe I would be disappointed if I really got to know him. Accepting this theory, I walked back to The Villas determined to call it an early night but a good one.

I woke up before sunrise the next morning. I had a to-do list as long as my right arm tacked to the billboard that hung over my desk. Still, I refused to cancel my plans to hang out with Tayo. I had promised and breaking promises was something we didn't do to each other.

It would take me at least a few hours to clean my room and

do the mountains of homework that I'd let pile up over the last week. I worked steadily without thinking about Duane, Kevin or the day with Tayo that lay ahead of me. I knew that if I took even a minute's rest to think about boys, I would get caught up in my thoughts, making it impossible to get anything worthwhile done. This determination worked to my advantage. I finished my to-do list in just over three hours. It was only a quarter past ten in the morning, plenty of time to primp and prep for someone who was just a friend.

Tayo and I made plans to see a midday showing of *Two Hearts*, a romantic comedy about a couple who fell in love only after being forced to celebrate their birthdays together. It was cheesy and poorly made, but that didn't stop us from laughing incessantly. My cheeks were aching, and I was sure that I'd received a complete two-hour abdominals workout as we left the theater.

"So you liked it, huh?" he asked as we walked back to his car, in stride with each other but at least a foot apart.

"Yeah, I guess I did," I admitted. Tayo had chosen the movie. The last thing I wanted to see was some silly, stupid movie about falling in love.

"Told you. You should listen to me more often, you know," he boasted.

"What's that supposed to mean?" I questioned with a laugh. But I knew that he was referring to the loads of advice about guys that he was always giving me. Apparently, I was too closed-minded, too hard to please. I was too impossible, so he said. I just didn't know how to lower my standards. And why should I?

"Nothing," he said with a smirk. He nudged me just hard enough to shake my balance. I did the same to him but with more force. We walked down the street taking turns pushing and pulling each other. Moments like these always warmed me to Tayo. My time with him was always easy, if nothing else.

"What are your plans for the rest of the day?" he asked, raising an eyebrow.

"I don't know yet."

"Spend it with me." He gave me his biggest smile. He always made it so hard to say no.

We spent the rest of the afternoon and that night in my dorm room, laying face up on opposite ends of my twin-sized bed. I let my crossed legs rest against his chest as I finally told him about Duane. He gave me his usual advice, and I showed my usual stubbornness.

"You rushed things. Your mistake," he said.

"I just don't like wasting my time. I'm not in the business of keeping guys who don't want to be kept," I said proudly. He moved my legs off of him and sat up to look at me.

"You're still trying to find the perfect Davis guy, aren't you?" It was more of an accusation than a question.

"So," I spat back, "what's so wrong with that?"

He shook his head with frustration. We had this conversation time and time again. Even more than believing me to be closed-minded and impossible, he thought it was silly for me to search for a Davis love. He said I was setting myself up for failure and that I needed to chill. Most of me agreed with him. I knew I was being ridiculous. I just couldn't help it.

"Plenty of guys are interested, you know," he said, moving to my end of the bed, placing his arm around my shoulder and drawing me in.

"You sound like you have a particular one in mind." I turned to face him.

He laughed. "You're not my type."

"Oh, really?" I teased. I knew that Tayo was attracted to me. It was the reason why we were friends. "So what's your type?"

"Well, let's see," he said after clearing his throat. "A lady in the streets but a freak in the sheets." I laughed even though I knew he was probably being serious.

"C'mon, Tayo," I said. "Really. I want to know. Humor me."

He pursed his lips, deep in thought. "My perfect girl?"

"Yeah."

"Smart. Funny. Nice body. Light-skinned. And she can cook."

Silence. I didn't know what to say, but I knew I had to say something. One small characteristic of his perfect girl had almost driven me to tears. Why light-skinned, I thought to myself. I was far from light-skinned, at least a shade or two darker than a chocolate bar, but I wasn't sure that my reaction had anything to do with *my* skin complexion. After all, I wasn't a good cook and yet that part of his perfect girl didn't bother me in the least. There was something operant that nagged about Tayo's perfect light-skinned girl.

"Why does she *have* to be light-skinned? Is there something wrong with my skin?"

I wondered why he was with me instead of Brianna. She was light-skinned with long curly hair. Why hadn't he asked DJ about *her*?

"No. You're very pretty. I tell you that all the time. You're sexy too," he said with a wink. "But, normally, I'm attracted to light-skinned girls."

This was something that I'd heard all too often although never from a friend. Some boys didn't see the problem in telling dark-skinned girls that they didn't like our skin and they would prefer us to be lighter. I had taken to ignoring the like. They were the reason why dark-skinned women around the world hated their complexion, with some even resorting to skin bleach.

My dark complexion had never bothered me, and I wouldn't let it start now. But that didn't stop the words of a friend from hurting me. I was even more hurt and annoyed because Tayo thought calling me pretty and sexy would make up for his ignorance.

"I know I'm pretty," I said. "And I love my skin, everything about it."

"You should," he said, smiling. "It's not that serious."

I rolled my eyes. I wasn't sure that I had the energy to explain the seriousness of it to him. I had the media indirectly calling light-skinned and mixed women beautiful everyday to compete with. Not to mention years of oppression.

"You'll never get it," I said. "I think you should go."

Maybe I should have taken the time to explain it to him. Maybe I sold him a dollar short. But I'd been there with guys before and I was sick of having the same, tired argument. Tayo was a mama's boy who didn't appreciate the image of his dark brown mother. If he didn't see the problem there, I didn't see how I could explain it to him.

I spent much of Sunday in my room. I just didn't want to bear another frosty January day. Instead, I lay in bed, letting the day pass me by.

Monday hit me in the face like a ton of bricks. I sat in my first two classes, clouded with thoughts of boys who continued to dishearten me. I wasn't fully awake until I heard the voice of my favorite professor.

Like a church sermon sometimes seems to bear witness to your life, my professor's lecture spoke to the questions that swirled in my mind as he explained the Manichean Order.

CHAPTER THREE: MR. NEW BOOTY

__Love wasn't in the statistics.__
__But was it in the room?__

"The Manichean Order impacts three major regions of self," my favorite professor explained. "It affects one's sense of competence, one's historical memory and one's body image."

I sat up straight to hear him further explain an order that divided the oppressed from their oppressor. Apparently, the oppression of my ancestors left more than the lingering remains of racism.

I looked around the classroom, wondering how many of us had a destructive sense of self. Do we doubt ourselves because we're black? How many thought lesser of their Davis education than one that they may have received at a traditional white school?

I thought about the uncle who reprimanded my decision to attend Davis, a historically black university.

"You have so many options. You're a smart girl. You did extremely well on your SATs. Don't sell yourself short," he'd said. Since when was going to one of the most prestigious universities in the country selling myself short? But maybe something resonated there.

Then there were my coworkers at the Genesis Group, a small ad agency that was providing two credits towards my graduation, who had no idea where Davis was located. The office was no more than twenty blocks from Davis' campus and kind of hard to miss.

Don't get me wrong, they ooh and ahh when you tell them you attend Davis University and congratulate you on going to such a wonderful school. But then they follow that with, "That's an African American school, right?" Had moments like those made me rethink my decision? Maybe I was battling my sense of self-efficacy.

There was also the comment from Tayo still gnawing at me about his perfect girl. His comment was a perfect demonstration of the Manichean mindset. I loved my dark skin. Or was that just what I told myself? Was I a product of this mindset as well?

As I pondered the effects of the Manichean Order, I took notice of an agreeing voice in my ear. I wasn't the only person completely immersed in the words of the professor. I turned around to see Greg sitting directly behind me.

"What are you doing here?" I whispered. "You're not in this class, are you?"

"No," he answered once the professor was silent. "I've already taken this course. He's great, isn't he? He's my mentor."

"Yeah, he's great. But, what are you *doing* here?"

"Oh, I have class in here next, well, now," he answered.

I looked at my watch to see that it was a couple minutes past one. Students shuffled around me, packing their bags.

Knowing that I'd missed my swift exit, I decided to wait around with Greg until his class started. I was at least eighty percent over Duane, but twenty percent was enough to continue avoiding him.

"So, what have you been up to lately? What's the latest good read?" I asked. Greg wouldn't know much about the latest rap song or the newest theater release, but he knew books. I always tailored my conversation to what he knew.

"Hmm. There's been a lot of them. I guess it just depends on what you're interested in. Are you reading anything interesting right now?"

"No, but I plan on starting *Black Skin, White Masks*," I said, without enthusiasm. I had no real desire to read it. I was only doing so because my favorite professor advised it.

"That's a good one. I think you'll learn a lot. I did. But it's clear that Fanon was no pseudo-intellectual. It's not an easy read."

"Yeah, I've heard that. That's why I've been putting it off."

He shook his head, unsatisfied with my abandonment of the book.

"Ok, class…" said his professor. It was my cue to leave.

Grabbing my books, I waved silently to Greg and headed for the door.

As I walked back to my dorm, I ran into Danielle. She was the first person I met at Davis, my roommate freshman year. That year we were the best of friends. Now, we'd accumulated new friends and were in completely different social circles, but we'd loosely held on to each other, saving time to catch up here and there.

"Kelly," she said in her usual, chirpy voice.

"Hey, Danielle. What's going on?" I asked looking up. At 5'10, Danielle had always towered over me. Her height complemented her thin figure. If she weren't so determined to be a doctor, she'd easily fit the bill of a runway model.

"Just life. Isn't it just gorgeous out here today?" She inhaled the chilly air around us.

"Yeah, sure," I said through chattering teeth. Leave it to Danielle to see weather that would usually cause people to curse as gorgeous.

"You know what?" she asked with excitement. "You should come with me to this event tonight." She held out a flyer that advertised, "The Other Side of The Fence."

As I read the description, I grew interested. It was a panel discussion on dating outside of your race. It was something that I'd never explored. Seeing that I was looking for my perfect love at an HBCU, there weren't many options outside of my race.

"I'm in," I said. "I guess I'll meet you at the main auditorium at seven."

"I'll be there," she said eagerly.

I hustled toward the direction of my dorm again. The weather was hardly gorgeous, and I was beginning to feel like a human popsicle.

At a quarter till seven, I walked up the hill to Kennedy Auditorium, a building that sat in the middle of campus, acting as the heart of Davis social life. All types of events were hosted there. The only place that drew more attention was the courtyard, the field of green that connected Kennedy, the Arts and Sciences library and a few lecture halls. The courtyard was often bare this time of year except during the rush between classes, but come spring students would sit outside on the courtyard all day and night. In the meantime, Kennedy would be packed with people.

I almost missed Danielle in the crowd. I finally found her in the back of the auditorium seated by... *Darius*! His slender six-foot-tall body coupled with his dark brown skin and well-groomed beard took me aback. His outfit was perfectly styled, his baseball cap turned backwards. I'd met Darius through Danielle freshman year. Not too long after, Darius and I had our moment. That's really all you can call it.

We never dated, yet there was some cosmic connection between the two of us. He was the guy that I couldn't wrap my head around. I'd tried ignoring him. I'd tried being friends with him. I swear that transcendental feeling for him was rock solid. Whenever we were in the same room, my eyes were his, just as my heart used to be.

Four years ago, I thought Darius was stalking me. What I never considered was that I might fall for him. How did *I* become the vulnerable one?

"Hey, Danielle, Darius," I said, approaching them and modestly taking a seat next to Danielle.

"Kelly," sang Danielle. Her singsong voice matched her wide eyes that smiled for her.

"What's up, Kelly?" asked Darius with a smirk. I'd had enough of that smirk. Sometimes I wanted to rip it right off of his face. That smirk somehow told me that I was transparent. Was his name written on the sleeve of my arm?

"Oh, not much," I answered shyly. He made me a little nervous. "How are you?"

"I'm good. Still standing."

"Same here, I guess." I smiled, and he gave me a little laugh. He could sense that I was uncomfortable. He found it amusing.

Luckily, we didn't have much time to chat. The event started promptly at seven o'clock. It began with a moderator who introduced the panelists and gave us all one fact to ponder.

"The number of available, educated black women far outnumbers that of available, educated black men," she said. "Black men are the second *most* likely ethnic group to date outside of their race, while black women are the *least* likely to date outside of their race. When you look at the numbers, they just don't add up. There are not enough black men to fulfill the unrelenting desires of black women."

I had only three-and-a-half months to find a man. Time wasn't the only thing not on my side. The numbers were against me. That, I knew. So I wondered why I'd walked to Kennedy in freezing weather just to hear the hammerhead hit the nail. But as I listened to the panelists, I began to ask myself the same question they were asking the audience. Why was I limiting myself? Worse than the skin tone preference, our men were ditching us for women completely different.

"Do the math. There will be black women who won't find the perfect black man. But if they choose to open their eyes to other options, they may find the perfect man," said one of the female panelists. She looked like she had a man somewhere, a sexy intelligent one at that. Her skin was glowing a deep mahogany.

I wanted to applaud her. I wanted to open my eyes to other men, but I had to be honest with myself. And honestly, I wasn't sure that I knew how to be completely happy with a man who wasn't black. I wasn't attracted to other men in the same way. Not because they didn't have black skin, but because there was something different about them. Maybe I thought the definition of a man was different for a black man than a man of any other race.

It was as if black men sat down their sons and gave them a secret and classified definition of a man. I saw this firsthand as I had an eighteen-year-old brother who seemed to have gone from being a boy to a man in a matter of weeks. He was no longer the little pest that would chase me around the house with a live cockroach in his hand, and I sure as hell couldn't beat him up anymore. Along with gaining muscle, he'd matured. He was more and more like my dad every day.

Black men seemed to carry this definition of a man everywhere they went. Walking with it, talking with it, surviving with it. Even the ones that didn't know their fathers were in on the secret. I didn't think their definition was any better or any worse than that of the other races, but it's what I grew to love about them. It's what I couldn't let go of. It's like the way Italian women from New Jersey seem to love their men juiced up and gel-friendly. I loved my men swagged out and black-defined. With that thought, I cursed myself for identifying with the cast of the Jersey Shore.

I tried to take in the message of the event, a fruitless effort. I'd come with an open mind but also a short attention span. I couldn't stop thinking about Darius. What was Danielle thinking? Sitting with him? She was always caught between the two of us, and today was literally no different. Every now and then, I would sit up or tilt my head back to see him through my peripheral. I only tuned into the discussion again in time to hear closing remarks. The event was over, and I would leave more close-minded than I'd come.

"Very interesting," mumbled Danielle. I could tell that she was working something out in her mind. It was the only time that she wasn't a ball of giggles and smiles.

The three of us walked out of Kennedy in silence. Maybe we were all deep in thought. Maybe we were all reminiscing about freshman year. Maybe that made things a little awkward and uncomfortable.

"Well, guys, I'm so glad that you came to the event with me. I never see you enough, Kelly," Danielle sang. I'd forgotten that she didn't live in The Villas like me and Darius. She'd be walking in the opposite direction to her room in Booker Hall. That meant that Darius and I had about a half mile's worth of alone time together. The thought in combination with the weather made me shiver.

"I know. We'll talk soon, maybe over lunch," I suggested.

"Sounds good," replied Danielle. "Bye, guys." Darius and I waved goodbye to her, then I turned to walk the path that ran through the center of the courtyard. I was quick on my feet, too quick for Darius, still facing Danielle's back.

"Wait up," he called. I'd lost my chance to run away, which is what my nerves were telling me to do. "You're quick." He laughed.

"Yeah, I'm just really cold," I lied. I tightened my arms against my chest, trying to be convincing. He laughed harder.

"A little body heat?" He held out his arms to me. His usual smirk ran across his face. This time I noticed that it was slightly crooked; it was forced. Maybe he was just as uncomfortable as I was.

"I think I'll make it. I'm just so over this season – winter. Spring never comes fast enough." That was my attempt at small talk. Weather was always a solid choice.

"I really miss hanging out with you, you know? I mean that," he said abruptly. If I wasn't frozen before, I was after hearing that.

"Hmm," I managed to get out.

Silence. Tell him that you missed him too. Tell him that there was something there, something here now. Silence.

"How's your sister? And your little brother?" he asked, changing the subject. The moment had passed just that quickly.

"They're doing alright. How are your brothers?" Darius was one of seven, smack in the middle of six brothers.

"Crazy," he answered.

Easy conversation filled the majority of our walk back to The

Villas, never returning to the statement Darius had made just minutes before.

It was as if we were freshmen again. The chemistry was still there. We were arguing over who had better taste in music when I heard a vaguely familiar voice call my name.

"You can't call yourself a music head when you don't have Outkast or KRS-One on your playlist," Darius squabbled. But I was too busy looking over my shoulder to make my usual retort.

In a matter of seconds, Kevin was at my right side while Darius was still hanging on to my left.

"W'sup, Kelly," he said. "Hey, man, what's up?" he acknowledged Darius. Darius and I both fell silent. I suppose Kevin was the only one at ease. "So, Kelly, I hear you're a math whiz," he continued.

"Well, I wouldn't go that far," I replied. In truth, I was a math whiz, naturally. My mother was a math teacher. It was in my genes.

"She told me you'd say that."

"She?" Before he could respond, I noticed that we were alone. Darius had disappeared somewhere between Columbia Avenue and the crossing to Madison Place.

"Brianna," Kevin answered. "I asked her about you."

I raised my eyebrows, an innate reaction.

"I need a math tutor. I asked her what you'd say," he clarified.

"Oh. Well, sure," I said. He'd asked about me. I was flattered, no matter what the reason.

We set a study date. Without the study part, it was just a *date*. I was excited to spend Wednesday afternoon with Kevin, even if over a stack of papers and his calculus book.

I sat in front of my thirteen-inch computer at my internship on Tuesday, counting the minutes instead of filling out the flow chart before me. If this were a real job, they would have surely fired me by now. I hated the work, and it showed. I was slow to turn in my assignments and quick to leave, never able to stay a minute past six o'clock. I was the only black intern, and there were only three black employees in the 100-person agency. I was afraid I was giving us all a bad name. Still, I couldn't stand being there enough to actually try since they only trusted the interns with busy work. I pretty much had a gig lined up after graduation at Neon Advertising in New York anyway. I interned for them the previous summer and got to work on a real ad campaign for Coca-

Cola. I left with a glowing recommendation and encouragement to seek them out after graduation.

As I thought about how great my life would be at Neon, the time slowly passed. What seemed like years later, I walked home.

Reaching my dorm room, there was one thing I had to do – figure out what I was going to wear on my study date with Kevin.

Tamika and I ransacked my wardrobe, picking out only the studious and sexy pieces. If Kevin was the one, I had to show him.

"I should just burn this wardrobe and start over," I complained. After searching for the perfect outfit for at least an hour, I was nothing short of completely frustrated.

"We'll find something. It's not like this is an actual date, anyway," she murmured.

"Heard that!"

"Well, it's true."

"That's what you say now. There have been a lot of guys, you know. But, there's just something about this one," I insisted. I don't know what inspired this resurgence of hope in me. I was ready to throw in the towel just a couple of weeks ago, but I had a good feeling about Kevin.

"You just met him. What makes this one so different?"

"It's the way he walks. He's confident. Even if he didn't know where he was, he wouldn't be lost. And he's funny."

"Hmm, I guess." She smiled as she held up a frilly, pink tunic. It was perfect, and this is why I knew she would be one of my bridesmaids someday. She was the clutch.

"Thanks," I cried. "Now I can finally get some sleep."

"That makes two of us."

I was well rested as I walked to the Arts and Sciences library the next day. It was fifteen minutes past five, which meant I was fifteen minutes late. I found that being a little late was often a good thing when it came to guys anyway. They should get used to waiting on us and not the other way around.

That I'd left my dorm room at all in this weather was a testament to my character. The snow was intense. It hadn't started but thirty minutes ago and already there was a sheet of white across the courtyard. If I were lucky, I would get snowed in with Kevin. Either that or I'd be trudging my way through ankle deep snow tonight.

I was wet and shivering from the snow when I walked into the library. So much for my outfit. But as I looked around the library, I failed to see Kevin's face. Would he stand me up?

"Kelly," I heard through a strong whisper.

I whirled around to see the pleasantly symmetrical face I'd been searching for. But, today he was different. He was wearing jeans and a sweater, a change from his usual sweats get up. And he was wearing eyeglasses. I was all too weak for a guy in glasses.

"This way," he said. He put an arm around me, and I was close enough to smell his cologne. I swooned, intoxicated by it. "I already put my books down."

"Oh." I hadn't noticed that he wasn't wearing a backpack or towing any books.

"How was your day?" he asked as we sat in front of a disorderly pile of books and papers.

"Not bad," I said nonchalantly. "It's snowing though," I added with excitement. I hated cold weather, but I loved the snow. My clothes were damp and uncomfortable. Still, I couldn't blame the snow.

"I guess that makes one of us that likes snow."

"You don't?" I asked accusingly.

"Not really. I'm from Chicago. I got over the excitement of snow years ago."

"Well, I'll love it for the both of us," I smiled. I thought I'd be nervous around Kevin. I wasn't. He was easy going. I didn't stutter or stammer like I sometimes would with Darius. Kevin exuded a cool that seemed to rub off on everyone around him. I thought back to the way he worked the crowd at Kyle's house.

"So maybe we should get started," he said.

"Sure. What exactly do you need help with?"

"Everything," he answered, opening the large blue book in front of us.

We started with linear functions and slowly made our way to derivatives. He actually wasn't horrible at calculus. It took only a few times of me explaining each theory for him to get it.

For the next hour or so, we kept to the books. The conversation didn't sway from Calculus 101. He asked. I explained. He regurgitated. I nodded. We moved through the book and his notes this way, rhythmically. It was hard to tell whether I was a darn good tutor or he wasn't bad at math, at all. We finally took a break after another thirty minutes of studying.

He stood up to stretch. I let my head rest in my hand as I watched him, adoringly so. He took off his glasses as he sat back down.

"What are you doing this weekend?" he asked. The question

surprised me.

"I'm not sure yet."

He played with the frame of his eyeglasses. I hoped that he was going somewhere with that question.

"What are you doing this weekend?" I prodded.

"My birthday's on Saturday. I'm having a party. I wouldn't mind if you came."

I smiled, happy that he'd invited me, sort of. As long as the roads weren't buried under snow, I'd make Tamika and Brianna go with me.

"I wouldn't mind going. How old will you be?"

"Twenty-one." I'd forgotten that he was a year younger than me. I guess I had to accept this one imperfection, his age. I had a traditional image of the perfect relationship. The guy was always older, taller and stronger. Two out of three wasn't bad when the pickings were slim. If nothing else, Kevin appeared to be mature for his age.

"Where are you having it?" I asked.

"I have a house. Well, I share a house with a few other guys and a girl. I thought you knew that. It's not too far from Kyle's house."

"Oh. I just assumed that you lived in The Villas." The night I ran into Kevin he was on his way to The Villas, like me. In fact, he'd walked in with me. We only separated at the elevators.

"I was visiting a friend," he said. Oh no. Some girl. He was visiting a girl. It was all too good to be true. "Xbox tournament," he clarified.

"Game junkie?" I asked, secretly relieved.

"Maybe a little. But there are more important things. I don't really have that much time for games." He gave me an implying look. Were we still talking about video games?

I was known to play a game or two with guys. But wasn't that the point? The cat chases the mouse. I had the role of the mouse down to an art though a time or two I'd found myself running a little too fast for the cat to catch me, to the point where he just gave up.

"What's taking up all of your time?" Sure, school was hard at times, but college had provided *me* with more time than high school ever had. Four or five hours of class were a full day. Throw in a few overnighters and that was the bulk of it.

"My job." He worked. Brownie points.

"Where do you work?"

"I work for the government. I'm an economics major."
"Wow. Econ. *You* should be tutoring *me*."
"You don't like economics? But it's all numbers. You should be great at it," he laughed.
"I don't have a problem with the numbers, just the concepts. And, hey, if it's just numbers and you like it so much, then what are you doing with a calculus tutor?"
He shrugged his shoulders. "I don't know."
"Hmm. Well do you want to get in some more studying? I have maybe another hour before I should be heading back." I really didn't even have that. I had a load of my own work waiting for me, but I was looking at this time with Kevin as an investment.
"Yeah. Sure." He put his eyeglasses back on.
Kevin closed the book not even twenty minutes later. He said that he'd crammed as much in his head as he could for the night. I started to clean up the scratch papers that were strewn across the table.
"You'll let me know if you need help again?" I asked.
"Yeah. I don't think I could find a better tutor."
I blushed.
As I finished cleaning the table, I looked out of the window to see what I was up against. There were about six inches of snow outside. At least classes would be cancelled tomorrow.
"I'll walk you back," he said. I hadn't noticed him beside me. We stood there looking outside the window, I in amazement and he in terror.
"Maybe we should get going," I suggested. He nodded, with a smile.
As we trekked through campus, we talked about our likes and dislikes, strengths and weaknesses. I was only half attentive. I was busy thinking about how great we'd look together. We fit well. I could feel it.
I went through our possible dates. What he would wear. What *I* would wear. The jokes we'd make together. The friends we'd go on double dates with. The people who would awe at how cute we were. Jealous girls. How I would describe him to my mother. How I would describe him to my *father*. Jealous guys. What our song would be. Where we'd have our first kiss. What he'd buy me for my birthday.
I'd completely forecasted our relationship by the time we reached The Villas. I walked ahead of him to the building's double doors.

Before I had a chance to go in, I felt a big thud on my back. I turned to Kevin, who was smiling guiltily. I hurried to pack a snowball of my own and hurled it at him. I missed. I tried again. Another miss. He ran toward me. A mixture of screaming and laughter exploded through me as he playfully knocked me into the snow. I reached for another snowball and with perfect aim I hit him on the head.

We laughed. But we didn't stop fighting. He was taking it light on me, but I was giving him my everything. I was a competitor, even in snow wars. We went on this way until I was completely soaked in snow and shivering.

"I guess I better go in," I said.

"Yeah." He laughed. He gave me a big hug. As he drew away he let his hand linger on the small of my back. I shivered again. Only it had nothing to do with how cold I was. He pulled away for good. "Don't forget about the party."

After saying goodbye to Kevin, I didn't go to my room. I had to tell Tamika all about him. Right now he was new, but he *could* be the one. And in addition to recounting my evening, detail-by-detail, I had to find the perfect outfit to wear to Kevin's birthday party on Saturday.

Talking to a new guy is always so exciting. Butterflies fill your stomach, your walk turns into a skip, and lame jokes are utterly hilarious. Brianna calls it, "new booty syndrome." Whatever you want to call it, I had it. What's a girl to do with a nose wide-open and blurry vision?

CHAPTER FOUR: DAD ALMIGHTY

*Love was piggyback rides. Hard-learned lessons.
Tickles and giggles. Unequivocal care.
And it all started with a little girl's father.*

Tamika sat still as I began to recount my evening with Kevin. Not a peep. Not a sound from her. I was having a conversation with myself, and it was a little awkward. Something was wrong. I tried to get it out of her.

"I'm fine," she said. "Really."

"We've lived in the same dorm for three years now. I spend way too much time with you. Half of my wardrobe is in your closet. You know what I'm going to say before I say it, and I know when you're upset."

A little chuckle, that was all she gave up. I'd have to try again in the morning. There was someone else I needed to talk to anyway.

I needed to talk to a guru, one of those girls who could get almost any guy she wanted. She's not necessarily beautiful. Beautiful girls are a dime a dozen. They have no trouble grabbing guys' attention. Retaining it is their problem. She isn't always the best dressed or the smartest girl, but there's something about her. Maybe charm. Maybe wit. Maybe I am way off the mark. Either way, she gets what she wants. She's the go-to girl when you need advice. And in this case, *she* was my mother.

My mother was the only one who didn't know how graceful and popular she was. Not only was she well proportioned with long hair and an attractive face that housed one deep dimple, but she was also dainty and feminine, having never played a sport in her life. That didn't mean she wasn't a sports fan though. She could sit in front of the TV watching ESPN and drinking beers with the best of them. She was like a playoff game and a Beyonce video all wrapped up in one. What guy would turn that down?

My father sure didn't. He was no slouch himself. To know him was to love him. He was the guy who couldn't leave the house without running into someone he knew. He never remembered their names, but he never forgot a face. He made best friends with the cashier who rung up his groceries, and he had over fifteen godchildren because he was always the perfect candidate for the job.

He and my mother were nearing their thirtieth anniversary. They were the perfect pair. He was the life of the party. She was the belle of the ball. They were the couple you couldn't help but hate.

"Kel, what are you doing calling here? Afraid I'd write you out of the will?" My dad laughed. If no one else would laugh at his jokes, he could always count on himself. But this time I pretended to laugh with him. Someone had to help convince him that he wasn't getting old and his jokes weren't getting lame.

"Nope. Dad, it's not even about the three dollars you're leaving me in the will today. Is Mom around?"

"Sorry Kelloggs." Kelloggs was one of the many nicknames my dad had given me as a kid and the only one that had really stuck although my little brother still called me Helter Kelter.

"Where is she?"

"In the shower." We both knew what that meant, a surge in the water bill and at least a thirty-minute wait on my end. It was as if my mother enjoyed being a prune.

"What do you need?" Dad asked bluntly. "Money? We're fresh out." Again, he laughed.

"No, I just wanted to talk to Mom. No big. I'll call back."

"Dear old Dad won't do, huh?" Oh no. He was in his feelings. I'd have to convince him that I enjoyed talking to him just as much as I liked talking to Mom.

"Not at all. Just girl stuff, you know."

"Well I've been married to a girl for twenty-nine years now. You're only twenty-two. Gotta mean I know more than you. That rhymed, eh? I sound like a rapper." I could tell that he wanted to laugh at his joke but was also trying to remain, to some extent, serious.

"Is that what it means?"

"Ok, Kelloggs. I'll just tell your mother to call you when she gets out of the shower. Guess I'm just not cool enough." What a guilt trip. He was showing me no mercy. At that point, I knew I had to tell him something.

"Well, there's this guy, you know? And he's cool. I mean, I like him. I think I like him. Yeah, I like him. I don't know him that well. But, there's something about him. I don't want to ruin things, Dad. I want to play my cards right. And Mom's the queen of poker. You know that. After all, she got you to chase her clear across country."

Thirty something years ago, my mother walked away from my father, her college sweetheart. I couldn't be sure why, but I had a guess. My mother didn't trust men, that much I knew, so it must have been hard for her to trust my party animal of a father. She moved all the way from Columbus, Ohio, to Atlanta, Georgia, to reinvent herself. It only took my father a month to follow her.

Years later and I still wasn't sure she trusted him. Whether my father had remained loyal was a mystery to us all, but there was one thing I was sure of: he loved her. He loved her with all that he had. It was an unconditional love, much greater than what she could reciprocate. Watching him love her had ruined me, turning me into a hopeless romantic and forcing me to believe in fairy tale romances because here they were, real living proof.

"So what do you think, Dad? What should I do?"

"Your mother was a star, Kelloggs. She was when I met her and she still is. I think you got some of that from her, some of that power, and you can use that. But even if you weren't a star in progress, I'd still say everybody's got a little light under the sun."

"Huh?"

"Everybody's got a little light under the sun." He said it again as if it would make more sense the second time around. "Really, it's that simple, Kelly."

And that was his advice. Well, I wasn't really sure that you could call it advice. I recognized the Funkadelic lyric from the song "Flashlight." My dad was a Parliament/Funkadelic/George Clinton enthusiast. I just didn't know what it had to do with me. Or Kevin. He tried to explain but I'd cashed out.

As he went on and on, I filed my nails, then searched for a new nail polish to wear Saturday night. Nails were important. Hands were important. Reaching for your hand was generally the first move that guys made when they were interested. Even if they were too scared to seriously go in for the handhold, they found a way to grab your hand and they studied it. "You have nice hands," or "they're so soft," or "I like your nails." And maybe, just maybe, he took your hand and intertwined it with his. So, you could see that hands were important. Nails were important. Which color?

"Kelloggs? Kel??" I'd completely missed him calling my name.

"Yeah, Dad?"

"Your mom just got out of the shower. I'm sure you still want to talk to her, right? You probably didn't hear a word I said." I knew Dad's feelings would be hurt if I asked to speak to Mom. I decided it best to skip out on that conversation. I would read one of those books on relationships instead – *The Art of Cat and Mouse* or *Finding a Man: The Basics*.

"No, Dad, you were actually really helpful."

"Well, what do you know?"

"I think I'm going to call it a night. Tell Mom I love her and I'll talk to her later."

Well that conversation was a bust, and I had no more insight than I'd started out with. I settled in to read a few chapters in *The Art of Cat and Mouse*. I didn't get much reading done. I was out cold before I was able to digest any of it.

I stared at my alarm clock in disbelief. It was ten minutes past nine, which meant that I was already ten minutes late for work. I checked my cell phone. Yep, the mistake was all mine. I looked outside, hoping to see enough snow to shut down the city. Nope, most of the snow had melted.

Somehow my night with Kevin had made me forget that I still had a life to tend to. I'd dreamed of sugarcoated candy, fragrant daisies, galloping unicorns, amicable pixies and deep-dimpled boys. I fought awaking to this sub-par reality, a fight that might put me in line for a lecture from the intern coordinator, seeing that it was my fourth or fifth time being tardy. "Professionalism, professionalism," she'd stress.

I was able to slip into my cubicle unnoticed forty-five minutes later. The day trudged along. I hadn't heard from Ms. Berry, the intern coordinator, and for that I was glad. But I wouldn't be fully cheery until I was at home picking out my outfit for Saturday night. Plus, I needed to make sure that Tamika was ok. It was hard to tell with her.

When six o'clock rolled around, I was relieved that Ms. Berry hadn't paid me a visit, and I wouldn't intern again for another four days. I had a little bit of homework to do but not enough to stress over.

After reaching The Villas, I didn't waste time going to my room. Instead, I took the elevator to the eighth floor to visit Tamika.

"Tamika." I didn't bother to knock. Payback. "Mika." I looked around the room. She was lying in bed. "Tamika!" I yelled, jumping on top of her. That woke her up.

"Whaaat?" she asked, startled.

"Hmm… Nothing. Just thought I'd tell you about our plans for Saturday."

"I don't care. Leave me alone," she squealed.

"Well," I started anyway, "Kevin invited me to his birthday party. You and Brianna have to go with me. Well, Brianna was probably invited herself, but that's not the point. The point is I'm expecting to have a very great Saturday. Of course, I'll need something to wear." I jumped up and walked to her closet.

"There's nothing in there. Leave me alone," she croaked, turning over and slamming the pillow on her face. Tamika was always such a grouch if she didn't wake up the natural way, which meant that she cursed her alarm clock every morning. After she caught on that I wasn't leaving any time soon, she sat up.

"Where are we going on Saturday?"

"Listen next time, and I won't have to repeat myself."

"You do want me to go, don't you? You'd think you'd be a little nicer, eh?"

"Kevin's house. He's having a birthday party. What do you say?" I said, ignoring her last comment.

"It sounds like it could be fun," she admitted. "Alright."

"I just have to figure out what to wear now. And should I get him a card? Or is that too much? We did just meet."

"Look in the second drawer. There's a blouse on top that you'll like. And no card. Too much, too soon. Just go. That says enough."

"Yeah, you're right. Hey, what was up last night? Is everything ok?"

She nodded, then smiled. "That time of the month." Something told me it was more, but I didn't question it. She would tell me in time. Often, being a friend meant just being there. Forcing her to dish wouldn't do anything but put an end to my curiosity. "Did something happen between you and Kevin?" she asked, her smile growing.

"Well..." If anyone could talk about a new guy as if he were the Buddha of Davis University – and by Buddha, I mean the guy from the reality series "I Love New York" – it was me. I had turned my study date with Kevin into a fictional tale of passion that could rival the start of any epic love story. But Tamika hung on to my every word.

We were so hyped that we were ready a whole two hours early on Saturday. We were ready before Brianna, who planned to meet us there, and that spoke volumes. We sat on opposite ends of my bed, twiddling our thumbs.

"Maybe we could go get a drink," I suggested.

"It's Saturday. No happy hour specials, and we don't want to show up drunk."

"Like that's not the norm. We're in college." We both laughed.

"I'm kinda hungry. Let's make brownies," squealed Tamika.

We made brownies to pass the time and relinquish the desire that *that* time of the month had brought Tamika. We were good and full of chocolate as we made our way to Kevin's house in search of even more chocolate. But this time, not the type that you devour so quickly.

Kevin's lanky and awfully goofy looking roommate, Rajean, greeted us at the door.

"Hey," he said, gawking at us with a champagne bottle in his hand. "More birthday girls," he called.

"Charming," was all I managed to say.

"Excuse me," Tamika said, as she grabbed my hand and led me under Rajean's propped up arm. We weren't five feet into the party when I realized how horrible this night would be. I was standing face to face with Darius. And even worse, he was talking to Kevin. What? Had they formed some type of I-hate-Kelly-Brown club? To my prior knowledge, they didn't even know each other. At least they didn't seem to know each other the night Darius and I ran into Kevin.

I managed a quick wave, but a dry throat didn't allow me to mutter a word. The nerves and anxiety that overcame me forced me past the two of them and into the kitchen where I reached for the nearest cup and gulped, not knowing whose it was or what it was. Some type of mixed drink, vodka. It was going to take another three or four of those to make this night bearable. Just as I reached for another cup of mystery punch, Kevin snuck up behind me.

"You made it!"

"Yeah. Happy birthday." Kevin handed me the cup I was reaching for and held his own to mine.

"To snowy nights. Drink up. You're behind." I smiled and took a sip. Here was this perfect guy standing before me, and I couldn't get my mind off of Darius. Darius was the first guy at Davis to truly catch my eye. Kevin's presence didn't have the same effect just yet. Though it could, in time.

Kevin looked great that night in his shrunk to fit Levis, hunter green button-down and the same black-framed eyeglasses he wore to the library. He looked different than the night I'd met him at the soiree. Somehow he'd managed to upgrade himself. He went from fine to FOINE!

Maybe he was even too good-looking. I didn't know how I'd ever find it possible to stand next to his perfection. That night didn't give me the chance to find out. He was so popular that he was always entertaining some new company, the perfect host. Every now and then, he would slide me a wink from across the room or brush past me, touching me just enough to make my insides tingle.

For the greater part of the night, I managed to duck and dodge Darius. And since Tamika and I'd arrived, he hadn't spent too much time with Kevin. Thank goodness. So maybe Darius was a friend of a friend, and they'd just met for the second time here at this party and hadn't had a chance to discuss a girl named Kelly Brown at all.

"Hey, Kelly." I recognized Darius' voice without turning around. It had a unique pitch. Freshman year, I couldn't get enough of it. It was higher than most guys'. But somehow he lost no masculinity there. He was a man in so many different ways. And he was so tall. Well, he was only six feet. But the way he raised his shoulders to tuck his hands in his jeans and the way he kept his chin tilted up elongated his body. He used every inch of his height to his advantage. I turned around to face him.

"Hey, Darius. What's up?"

"Cool party. How do you know Kevin?"

"I'm his math tutor." I giggled. Like always, Darius turned me into a little girl – the shy girl who giggles when her crush says hi to her.

"I didn't know you were that good at math," he said with his usual smirk. It always made me think that he knew something I'd missed. Did I have birthday cake on my face? I took a quick swipe at my mouth before answering.

"There's a lot you don't know about me."

"I wouldn't say a lot." The words came out as if he knew my secrets. It was as if he'd seen me naked. Darius had *never* seen me naked.

"Hey, do you want to grab something to eat sometime?" Did those words just come out of my mouth? What was I thinking? Darius was the last guy I should be asking out. And in what way was I asking him out? My mouth diarrhea made me think about the conversation I had with my dad the other day. I walked away before he could answer.

My dad hadn't told me much. He'd shown me. He'd shown me the possibilities. I wouldn't settle for anything less than what my mother had. Why chase after some guy when I could wait for the one that would chase me clear across the country? Maybe that's what he meant after all. Heeding his advice, I chose to wait for the fairy tale. My star was still in progress.

I left the party early. On my way home, I found myself reminiscing about freshman year, Darius and this intriguing city.

CHAPTER FIVE: MR. DOBERVILLE

Was Doberville the love of my life?

There was something about Doberville, Maryland, that I loved. Whatever drew me there, kept me there like a lover that I longed for. And even more like a lover, I ached for this city. Everyone in Doberville looked older than they ought to. They'd all weathered something, and it showed on the surface of their skin. The rodents that ran rapid, the crime rate, the STD statistics and the beggars on every corner all contributed to their early aging.

I met Doberville when I arrived in the heart of it to attend Davis. Since then, I had come to realize that Doberville wore more than just its problems on its sleeve. It was an external place. The beauty and the persistence of its people all shown clear as the sun in Doberville – from the teenage boy who played his violin for money in the acoustically brilliant tunnels of the public transit system to the go-go music that the city seemed to breath and thus could be heard blaring from shops and residences on most street corners.

That was what I loved about it. Not to mention, who didn't love a complete badass? Doberville was one badass city, and I was drawn to it like a Catholic schoolgirl swoons over a bad boy with a motorcycle.

As I walked through the city that night, I found myself clutching tightly to my pepper spray and looking from corner to corner for any signs of danger. I remembered the repetitive warnings and haunting stories of administrators and resident assistants about walking around Doberville. "Do not wander alone. Avoid these streets even in daylight. Take the campus shuttle."

But there was something in me that wanted to trust my people. African Americans made up 92 percent of Doberville's population. Why should I be scared of the brown faces around me that resembled my mom, dad, sister, brother and friends? That logic, however, didn't stop the creeping fear that prickled my spine as I made my way home. After all, it was a stupid rationalization, "my people."

As my favorite professor had once said to our class, "The disparities are real." The crime rate on this side of town really was higher. There really was reason to be fearful.

I faced the ugly fact that things weren't easy over here, while remembering to put it all in context. The neighborhood wasn't bad and neither were the black people who lived in it. It was all circumstantial. Years after slavery, and the community's circumstances still weren't at their best. Windows were barred. Bulletproof glass stood between you and the local bank tellers. Police sirens were more frequent than the sound of chirping crickets. We still had a lot to overcome, but our color wasn't a part of that lot.

I was close to reaching my dorm, and with each step feeling a bit more secure about my surroundings. It was a cold night, and I longed for the warmth of my room. But at the same time, I enjoyed walking through this city. It gave me time to think and made me feel free, knowing that the city had so much to offer me.

I took in the night air. With each breath, I could feel the city's personified being. The wind's heartbeat made me think of the people here: the little old lady who sat next to you on the bus, the kids who all looked and dressed years older than they should, and the bickering men and women who solved their arguments with coarse laughter. These people were warm, and I was comfortable around them.

And then there was Darius, Mr. Doberville. Sometimes I didn't know whether I'd fallen for the city or for him freshman year. Maybe the city was all I could have of him. It was so much of him... or he was so much of the city. Fitted jeans, feet beating, go-go records, external emotions, outgrown beard, loud mouth, quick wit, Doberville swag. But I couldn't trust him anymore than

I could trust the Doberville streets. He was often as cold as the windy, wintry nights. But like I could never hate the snow, like I could never hate the city, I could never hate him.

Darius was no longer the boy I met freshman year. He'd changed. Again, it was the effect that Davis had on boys. One year at Davis and they all thought they were the shit. But I liked to remember the outspoken boy I met freshman year, the one who would call me over and over until I picked up the phone.

I met Darius through Danielle on October 27, 2006. The date stood out because it was my nineteenth birthday. I'd gone out to dinner with friends and ran into Danielle, who'd just gotten off work, on our way back. I actually couldn't recall the faces of the two guys she introduced me to that night, but according to Darius, he was one of them. He claimed to remember me smiling.

The first thing I remembered about him was the African pageant. He was Mr. Nigeria, or maybe Mr. Kenya. I couldn't remember which of the two. Either way, he was awful. Danielle pointed him out to me.

"There's Darius. In the purple. He's been talking about this pageant all week."

"How do you know him again?"

"We have class together."

I knew one of the other contestants, Malik. I focused most of my attention on him, Mr. Eritrea. Unlike Darius, he was poised and charismatic. When the talent portion came around, Darius lost all chance of success. He sang Al Green's "Simply Beautiful," a song I wasn't too familiar with and frankly never wanted to hear again after Darius' rendition. To say that he was a bad singer would be a drastic understatement.

"He's awful," I whispered to Danielle.

"Shhhh." She was determined not to betray her friend with harsh words though she couldn't stifle a small giggle. After the pageant ended with Malik receiving his crown, we waited for Darius. Danielle wanted to give him a pat on the back.

"You were great," she lied.

"Yeah. Thanks," he said, a little forlorn but still with a smile. "I thought I would at least place." I thought he should have been grateful that they hadn't kicked him off of the stage, but I kept quiet. Later that night, Darius came to visit Danielle in our dorm room. Only a few floors separated our rooms in Booker Hall.

"Hey. Thanks again for coming," he beamed. He was awfully happy for a guy who had just made a fool out of himself in a very public pageant.

"Sure, boo," Danielle sang.

"What are you two doing tonight?"

"We're staying in. We're losers," she answered. "What are you doing?"

"I'm going out to dinner with my family. I guess I'm a loser too. They're actually waiting for me so I gotta go. I just wanted to thank both of you for coming." Maybe that was the first time he'd caught my attention. He wanted to thank *both* of us, and I didn't even know him.

"What's his name again?" I asked after he left the room.

"Darius," Danielle said, a little frustrated with my forgetfulness.

"He's nice. He can't sing, but he's nice. Do you like him?"

"No, we're just friends." Four years ago, I didn't know Danielle quite as well as I knew her now. She was into athletes. Though Darius played basketball in high school, he was not your typical jock. He didn't look the part or act the part. He was too well groomed and didn't have one piece of Davis Athletics paraphernalia. They really were *just* friends.

"He thinks you're pretty," she said.

So many guys would tell Danielle that they thought I was pretty and so many would tell me that they thought she was. Freshman year hormones ran wild. Everyone looked good to everyone. As the years passed, we picked each other apart until only a small fraction seemed worth the effort to entertain. The flowerpot looked full until you pulled out all of the weeds. Now, my ears would perk up when a guy called me pretty. But then, I didn't pay it much mind, at least not until we met again a week later in the cafeteria.

The cafeteria was the best and the worst back then. Every freshman would be there between the hours of six to seven for dinner. It was best to make arrangements so that you could meet a friend there at exactly the same time. Being caught alone was social suicide. Even if you got your food before your friends did, you would linger around until they were ready to sit with you.

Aside from the stress of finding a seat among friends, going to the cafeteria would often be the best part of the day. Students would miss class chilling in the cafeteria. And sometimes DJ would be there, playing music from every hometown. The Midwest. The Caribbean. Down South. California Bay Area. New York. Everyone had a song to dance to and a hometown to represent.

This one particular day, I showed up to the cafeteria alone. Not to worry, Danielle had saved me a seat at her table. I found her quickly, sat my book bag in the seat next to her and left to pick up a food tray. As I reached for one of the red trays, still damp from being washed, I bumped into Darius.

"Hey," I said. I still couldn't remember his name.

"Hey. It's Kelly, right?"

"Yeah." He walked away, but my eyes followed him to his seat across from Danielle. "It's Kelly, right?" I snickered under my breath. Why act like you're uncertain of my name, I thought. But something about that was really cute, in the same way that thanking me even though I didn't know him was.

After I got my food, I sat at the table with Danielle, Darius and a few other friends. It was then that our moment began. How we got on the subject of dating I don't know. It was so often the topic of conversation.

Back then, everything seemed so simple. I thought that there wasn't a guy that I couldn't wrap around my finger. I played all types of little tricks and games to get my way. And often, it worked. I revealed a little bit of this to the table and from that point on, Darius couldn't keep his eyes off of me. Whether or not I enjoyed him in the same way is debatable, but I certainly didn't mind the attention I was receiving.

"If you tell someone they like you, they will," I said, while eyeing Darius. "All you have to do is tell them."

"Things are always more complicated than that, Kelly," Danielle said.

"Things are complicated because we make them complicated."

"Jedi mind trick?" Darius questioned. "I don't know." That was the first time I saw the smirk. He could play just as many games as I could.

"It's not a trick. You just have to put the thought in someone's mind. You can't like someone you don't think about."

"But there are plenty of people who you think about but don't like," he retorted.

"Not often," I said with a smile. "If you think about them often, there's a good chance you like them. No matter if you want to admit it or not."

"Who do you think about?" he laughed.

"My mind is blank right now."

"Smart girl."

Playful banter always makes for an interesting start, but it didn't last long. Darius and his friend Gerry left the table first, and Casey – a friend I'd made in a freshman English class – and I not too long after. Casey wanted to go to a freshman poetry cipher being held in her dorm. I agreed to go with her.

The cipher was nearly finished when we walked in. The poems that we did get a chance to hear ranged from lengthy, rhythmic raps about life to short haikus about love. Spoken word. It was a mix of music and poetry. The poet would slow down or speed up his lyrics to convey an emotion. Even words like "was" and "him" carried weight when isolated and drawn out. "And he waaaaas the metaphysical being of hiiiiimself." Sometimes, I understood the message. Other times, I didn't. But the musicality of it never failed me.

Casey and I parted ways after the cipher as she went to her room, and I began the short walk back to my dorm, which was on the other side of the courtyard. I was a few steps out the door when I heard someone call my name.

"Kelly, wait up." I turned around to see Darius jogging to catch up with me. "You shouldn't walk alone. It's getting late."

"Sure," I teased.

"So you're into poetry," he said. I had eyed Darius at the cipher.

"A little. Casey wanted to go, so I told her I would tag along. I guess you're into poetry though. That or the cipher was just an excuse to visit an all-girls dorm." He just laughed.

"Where are you from?"

"Atlanta. You?"

"I'm from here. Doberville."

"Oh no. So that must mean that you beat your feet and listen to all of that silly go-go music."

"Yep. See the slits in the bottom of my jeans? That's a Doberville thing." I looked down to see the inch-high slits that were cut right along the seams of his pants. "There's nothing wrong with go-go. I bet you haven't even heard that many songs."

"Well, 'Sexy Lady' is the only song that I like." Davis didn't exactly associate itself with Doberville. In fact, it rejected some of the major representations of the city, like go-go music. You wouldn't hear that type of music at a Davis function. But you would hear "Sexy Lady." It was the one new era go-go song that had crossed over. The only other songs to get play were classics like "Da Butt."

"Let me see your iPod," he said. I shot him a skeptical look but withdrew the small white music player from my handbag. He quickly scanned the songs. "Interesting playlist. Not too much music from Atlanta in here."

"Yeah, my friend from California gave me a ton of music. That's where a lot of it comes from."

"I'll update it for you." He shrugged. We'd reached the door of our dorm. Darius handed me my iPod and shot ahead of me to his room. "I'll meet you in your room. I'm going to get my computer," he called back.

I didn't know what to think of Darius as I entered my perfectly square dorm room. Danielle and I had divided it in half. An imaginary line was drawn right down the middle of the room. The blue and green decorated right side belonged to me, while the pretty in pink side was Danielle's. She sat on her ruffled pink covers, texting.

"Branden?" I inquired. Danielle and Branden, a rookie football player, had an interesting friendship freshman year. It was one of those flirty, tickle me pink friendships that made everyone else think that it was something more.

"No," she said. "Kiara is having a party. She wants us to come. Wanna go?"

"Sure. Why not? I have to wait for Darius though. He's coming by."

"To see you?" she questioned.

"Just to update my iPod," I clarified. Not a moment later, there was a knock on the door.

"Come in," I called. Darius walked in with a computer, an iPod and an assortment of cords. "You're not moving in here, you know?"

"I'm considering it." There was that smirk again.

"What do you have for me?" I said, holding out my palms like a kid on Christmas day.

"Any song you want. I'm a music buff. I have everything."

"Hmm, I'm not really sure what I want. You can decide for me."

"Ok." Darius began to situate his things.

"We're actually heading out, Darius. Maybe you can just give me my iPod when we get back?"

"Sure." He regained his belongings. "Where are you going?"

"Our friend is throwing a party," Danielle answered for me.

"I can't go," Darius said.

"Well, we didn't exactly invite you," I said.

"You're not so nice, you know? But, I will take your number."

I raised my eyebrows in question.

"That way I can call you when I'm done with your iPod." The explanation allowed me to let down my guard and give him my number. Not too long after, Danielle and I left for Kiara's party.

We were among the first to arrive at the party. The music was already bumping, and she'd cleared the living room of the couch and coffee table that had formerly decorated it. I also noticed a pole in the middle of the room.

"Kiara, did you know that there's a stripper pole in your house?"

"Yeah, it was here when we signed the lease. It should make the night interesting though."

"Who's up first?" Danielle giggled.

"Not me," I said, simultaneously moving away from the pole.

It didn't take the party long to get started. Within the hour the crowd consumed the dance floor, spilling out of the living room, into the kitchen and onto the stairwell that led to the bedrooms above. The larger the crowd became, the more I began to feel woozy. The loud music was giving me a throbbing headache, and I wasn't sure how well my stomach was coping with the cafeteria food I'd eaten earlier that evening.

"Kiara, do you mind if I lie down for awhile? Danielle seems to be having fun, and I don't want to leave without her, but I'm not feeling too well."

"Are you ok? I have some Tylenol."

"No, I'm ok. I just need to lie down."

"Sure. Sure. My room is upstairs. First door on the right."

I slowly made my way through the crowd on the steps and into Kiara's messy bedroom. I plopped on top of coats strewn across the bed and closed my eyes. But falling asleep was impossible as my headache only intensified. I thought about finding Kiara to take her up on that Tylenol offer but I didn't think I could handle fighting through the crowd again. And something was vibrating. Then I remembered I'd put my cell phone in my back pocket. I looked at the caller ID. Darius.

"Mmm," was all I managed to say.

"Kelly?"

"Yes, it's me."

"Why do you sound like that?" he laughed.

"Music... too... loud... headache." I'm known for being slightly dramatic when I'm not feeling well.

"Well, I hope you're ok. I finished updating your iPod."

"I'll call you... when I'm in the dorm." I hung up and somehow fell asleep. I awoke to shuffling feet around me. People were trying their best to leave with the coat they'd come with without waking me, or worse, knocking me off the bed.

"Oh, sorry." I instantly sat up. I saw Danielle sitting in the chair beside the bed, patiently.

"Well, weren't you going to wake me?" I fussed.

"You just looked so peaceful."

"Let's go," I said as I rolled my eyes.

Not far from the dorm, I remembered that I told Darius that I would call him. I had four missed calls and two text messages. All from Darius. He wanted to know where I was and if I was ok. And maybe I should've found this sweet, but on the contrary, I was a bit creeped out. I mean he called me four times! Four times after I said I would call him back. Maybe I *already* had my hands full with this guy. Next week he'd be stalking me. So I didn't call Darius back that night.

I woke up the next morning to an empty room. Danielle had gone home to Virginia for the weekend. It was Saturday morning, and I had no plans for the night. I didn't leave my room much that day. Instead, I sat around reading and listening to the radio. That is, until I heard a knock on my dorm.

It was Darius, of course.

"What are you doing?" he asked.

"Reading."

"Reading what?"

"*Their Eyes Were Watching God*. It's my favorite."

"You're kidding. Mine too. I even thought about going to Howard because it's Zora's alma mater."

"Yeah, it's a classic. But I'm sure you didn't come here to talk about Zora Neale Hurston. You brought my iPod?"

"Yes, but that's not why I came either."

"It's not?"

"No, I want you to eat with me. Let's go to the cafeteria."

"Sorry, Darius. I'm not really in the mood. I just want to stay in."

"Please. Come on." He was pleading, and it was cute. He was cute. He was smirking. But, I still didn't intend to leave my room.

"Go without me," I whined.

"Well you don't get your iPod until I come back." I giggled as he turned his back and headed out of my room.

Darius came back just under an hour later. This time, he had my iPod, his iPod and a DVD in tow.

He stood in the door waiting for the invitation to come in that I had not given him yet. Really, I didn't want company. I just wanted my iPod back.

"Can I have my iPod now?" I asked without enthusiasm.

"Can I come in?"

I opened the door a bit wider, allowing him to accept the unspoken invitation. He handed me my iPod and sat down on my perfectly made bed. I peered at him with raised eyebrows.

"Would you rather I sit on the floor?" he asked.

I rearranged my face and began to browse the songs in my newly updated iPod. For a while we sat in silence as I read through familiar song names. Darius had only given me four new songs, and odd songs at that. The theme song from Home Alone, "I Wanna Be Your Man" by Zapp and Roger, "Sexy Lady" by UCB and a song by Andre 3000 from the "Idlewild" soundtrack. At the time, I didn't know what to think of Darius' selection of these mysterious four songs. The theme song from Home Alone? But to this day, they remain on my iPod because they represent everything that I grew to love about him.

"You only added four songs."

"I know."

"Let me rephrase. Why did you only add four songs?"

"Well I don't know what you like to listen to."

"But you assumed that I would want to listen to the theme song from Home Alone?"

"It's a good song."

"That's sorta beside the point. Can I see your iPod?" I asked, hand outstretched.

The iPod that Darius handed me was more than a little beaten up. It was a miracle it actually worked. Even the black case that hadn't done much to protect it was battered and torn. But it had a multitude of songs from varied artists. He had jazz ("In a Sentimental Mood"), rhythm and blues (old and new), rap (KRS One and Andre 3000 of course), pop (the songs you'd hear on the most popular radio stations), and songs by groups like Queen that I didn't know exactly how to categorize. He really was a music buff, and he really did have everything.

"Can I keep it?" I joked. "You have a lot of good music on here."

"So you trust my taste in music then?"

"You could say that."

"Then here, let me play something for you." Darius reached for the iPod and scrolled through the songs. After finding what he had been searching for, he moved in a bit closer to me as I had sat down on the bed next to him and gently placed each headphone in my ears – the left in the left and the right in the right. I listened to a go-go song that to this day, I can't find in iTunes or on Youtube. I even tried to explain it to DJ once, a failed attempt. Maybe it's because the only way for me to describe it is to describe him.

As I listened to this song, Darius searched my face as if to find every piece of enjoyment or criticism that might seep through it. And at this point, I knew he'd won. I didn't hate go-go because I didn't hate him. I was into it and I was very quickly becoming into him. I abruptly removed the headphones. I couldn't allow Darius to read my face any longer, lest he see the emotion ridden all over it. As I handed the headphones back to him, I realized that we were awkwardly close. Our knees were touching.

"Well, did you like it?" Darius questioned as I moved a few inches away from him.

"Sure, it was alright," I answered nonchalantly.

"Keep my iPod for a while. That way I'll have time to add a few more songs to yours." When I handed my iPod back to him, he closed his hand around mine. For a few seconds, he sat in silence and I in confusion. But he didn't let my hand go and I hadn't released his either.

"You like holding my hand," he said. I wasn't quite sure whether that was a question or a statement. Jedi mind trick? I took my hand back, trying to seem indifferent.

"So what DVD did you bring?" I asked, changing the subject. A smirk slid across his face.

"*The Wiz*. I've had it for years, but I've never seen it."

"You've never seen *The Wiz*?" I asked in shock. I practically grew up easing down the road with Diana Ross as Dorothy and Michael Jackson as the scarecrow. If you didn't grow up singing, "He's the wiz and he lives in Ozzzz," you've missed an important element of childhood.

"Never."

"Well, then," I said, picking up the DVD and putting it in the player.

It didn't take much for Darius and I to get comfortable. We started the movie, not touching, lying head to foot on my small bed. A simple joke about stinky feet turned Darius around, and for a while we just lied there next to each other. I lay on the interior of the bed against the wall and he on the exterior. Suddenly, he moved closer, smashing me against the wall and putting the pressure of his body against mine.

"Hey," I said, laughing. "Look at all of that room you have. Move over." He ignored me and pretended to be asleep. "Darius," I continued, prodding him.

He turned toward me and looked me in the eye. His stare went right through me to the core of my body, making my stomach flip. He smoothed down the hair that ran past my shoulders and down my back, then he focused his attention on my face.

"Your eyebrows are so thick. I like them," he said. As he admired my face, I admired his, running my fingers along his ear and over his fade. His eyes were deep set, giving him a permanently intense look, and his dark chocolate skin contained no flaws. He had a lot of facial hair including a small growth of a beard, but his wide smile balanced out what would've been a hard exterior. It all fit. Our hands together. Our noses. Our eyebrows. Our legs intertwined. We fit.

At around four in the morning, Darius remembered that he had to go to work in three hours. He worked at a Radio Shack not too far from campus. So he left me alone, with his iPod and thoughts of him. I let the music rock me to sleep.

Darius and I were drawn to each other for the next couple of weeks. So much so that we never said goodnight or goodbye. Our text messages were one long stream of conversation. We never went so far as a kiss, but I couldn't see how anything, not even a kiss, could bring me much closer to him. Not until I realized that I wasn't the only one close to him.

Darius and I were headed to McDonalds for a late night snack before another one of our movie nights. It was then that he said frankly, "You know I have a girlfriend, right?"

I hadn't known, and how would I? My heart could've dropped right out of my chest and onto the floor. I couldn't reply, lest I define myself a fool.

"I didn't think that I would come here and find someone like you. I never thought I would. I couldn't have imagined you. I like you a lot," he said.

"Would you say that in front of your girlfriend?" I asked.

"I'm not stupid."

"Then maybe you shouldn't say it at all."

We went to McDonalds that night, and we watched the movie.

And believe it or not we enjoyed ourselves, much in the same way that we did when we watched *The Wiz*.

But in the back of my mind, I knew. I knew that things would go downhill from there.

No, Darius and I didn't have sex. We never even kissed. But in many ways, I was giving him so much of me. We were always preoccupied with each other. By Thanksgiving break, I'd met most of his friends and he most of mine. And his friends would watch me. If they were around to see a different guy try to talk to me, they were there to intercede like the United Nations. After my plans to date a new guy fell through, Darius teased me, happy that the competition had failed. But I could never quite understand him or why he seemed so pleased when romantic entanglements didn't work out for me. He had a girlfriend after all.

Darius always called and stopped by. And his wide smirk and straight forward conversation made it impossible for me to not like him. I was enjoying, but at the same time resenting everything about him. How could he be so open? Why wouldn't he keep his eyes off of me? How did he know every song ever recorded? Why did he have perfectly white teeth? Why was he the only person I wanted to talk to at the end of the day? And why, why, why did he have a girlfriend? Where was the space for me?

Coming from Atlanta, I'd only known one type of guy. From 2004 to 2006, Atlanta boys really did only wear long white tees, and they really did lean and rock with it all day. Every guy from Atlanta owned a pair of Air Force Ones and a Braves cap, and they sagged their pants super low. Don't get me wrong, I loved Atlanta boys, but they all seemed to be cut from the same mold. Meeting Darius was like a breath of fresh air. I was relieved to breathe him. It was addictive.

Before I could blink twice, Christmas break marked the close of my first semester at Davis University, and I returned home to Atlanta. The last couple of weeks before the break, I began to draw away from Darius. I didn't have it in me to be the other woman, and over the break, I completely made up my mind to put an end to our undefined relationship.

Darius called me on Christmas Day. I didn't know how to tell him that I couldn't be his friend anymore, that it hurt to be around him, that I wanted him to leave his girlfriend. So instead we talked about our Christmas gifts and the feasts that filled our bellies. As I listened to this mindless chatter, I thought of how wrong Darius was for me. I tried to convince myself of how embarrassed

I would've been to call him mine at the African Pageant. But I was breaking and I knew it, so when my mother forced me off the phone and he asked me if I would call him back I said, "No," and hung up.

When we got back to school, I completely ignored him. He couldn't even get a "hello" out of me. Funny that I would later find out that he and his girlfriend broke up over the Christmas break, and only crazier would our story become over the next three years. But now, when I sit back and think of my Mr. Doberville, I wonder if I really fell for him or just for the city that raised him. That was a question I might never know the answer to. I met him at the very same time as that badass city and often mixed up the memories of the two.

That night after Kevin's party, I went to sleep, half tipsy and wondering what Darius meant to me. What seemed like only moments later, I awoke to Tamika pounding on my door. Maybe I'd missed some juicy gossip due to my early departure the night before.

CHAPTER SIX: THE DJ

*Often we associate love with whom,
but sometimes it comes in the form of a what.*

Girlfriends gave the worst guy advice. They were so hopeful, and they pushed all of that hope into your heart. When those hopes didn't materialize, you were left not just alone but hopelessly alone.

For this reason, I always kept a male friend in my corner. I put his number on speed dial so when my girlfriends made over some new guy in my life, he'd be there to bring me back down to Earth. That friend, so important to me, was DJ.

DJ was the perfect guy. He was the guy who never really had to apologize, but he did if he thought he hurt you. He would find you a cough drop or a piece of candy if you said your throat was itchy. He never forgot to buy you a drink on your birthday. And he personalized his Happy Thanksgiving and Merry Christmas text messages. He was easy to talk to and so much fun to be around. It didn't hurt that he had a smile worth dying for. Two deep dimples.

Had I not put DJ in the friend category early on, I may have found myself head over heels for the guy. But DJ wasn't the kind of guy who you could love. Or at least he wasn't the kind of guy who you *should* love because he would never be able to reciprocate those feelings.

I believed that each heart could only exert so much love, and that you chose what you poured your heart into. Some time ago,

DJ chose music and he never let it go. So I wasn't too surprised by the news Tamika shared with me that Sunday morning, but I felt for her. And there was also the guilt because I *had* introduced them.

"DJ and I aren't talking anymore." For a while, we were both silent. "Some girl. Some other girl," she said quietly, almost a whisper.

"Don't do this to yourself again," I said. DJ and Tamika had fought about "other girls" and "other guys" since they'd started dating. They cared for each other even if he wasn't capable of love. Everyone knew it. So this "other girl" was most likely just your typical, everyday, run of the mill... whore.

"This girl has made one too many. I'm sick of waiting on him to only need me. I only date other guys because he wants to date other girls. I told him... I told him I loved him, Kelly."

Because DJ was incapable of loving her, he was also incapable of monogamy and commitment. It wasn't hard for me to see, but it was hard for me to say. I was a typical girlfriend, hopeful, even though I knew the reality.

"What did he say?"

"That he loves me, but he's not in love with me."

"Tamika, I can only imagine how you feel right now, but I honestly think that DJ just needs time. It's not about the other girls. It's about his music. Right now, his music has his heart."

"That doesn't make it hurt any less."

I couldn't fully say I knew how she felt. I'd never used the words "I love you," let alone felt the intensity behind them. But I did understand jealousy, and it didn't matter whether a girl stole your man or an artistic interest did the dirty deed. Either way, you were without. Tamika was jealous of the love DJ had for music, the love he didn't have for her.

"Do you know why I left the party early last night?" I asked.

"No, though I have to admit that I was a little annoyed that you ditched me. You left me with Brianna," she laughed. "You know how crazy she is."

"Yeah," I nodded. "Sorry about that. But I asked Darius out. The words just flew out of my mouth." Tamika sat in shock. "I think it's easy to chase someone who is just out of reach. You start to think: just one more step and I'll have him. But it doesn't work that way. As long as he knows that you're interested... well, you've done your part and that's all you can do."

"That doesn't make it any easier." She shook her head.

"But this does. Girlfriends do. Best friends do. We're in the same boat here. Take comfort in that."

I knew my talk with Tamika wouldn't heal her wounds. Only time would do that. And maybe DJ would come around. As a hopeful girlfriend, I had to believe in the possibility.

My hope dwindled after speaking with DJ. He turned to me for advice, just as I turned to him. I heard his side of the story that Sunday evening.

"Hey, Deej. What have you been up to? Other than breaking hearts."

"You know I didn't mean to hurt her, Kelly." He walked in my room and took a seat in my desk chair. I sat, Indian style, on my bed across from him.

"Yeah. Well, in this case, intentions don't mean a whole lot."

"I know. I couldn't say, 'I love you.' It would be dishonest." He fingered the headphones he had in his hands.

"I wish you would open up and give yourself the chance to fall in love. Don't get me wrong, music is great. I love music. I spent most of my adolescence in my room, listening to music. I get it. But your music will never love you back. And you'll never be good enough. That's just how that type of passion works. It's one sided."

We sat in silence for a while. Just when I thought he was coming around, he got up.

"There's someone else," he said, emphasizing the word someone.

"Someone?" I asked in disbelief. "Let's not bring your whores into this. How a college DJ has groupies, I will never understand," I said, rolling my eyes. "No offense, of course."

"None taken," he laughed. Quickly, he grew serious again. "She's not a whore. I like her... a lot." He finally set the headphones down.

I'd known DJ since freshman year and had never heard him put the "a lot" after mentioning a girl who he liked. I was perplexed. He hadn't told me about any other girl. This nameless girl had appeared out of thin air – as they often do.

"DJ, you've never even mentioned..." I waited for him to fill in her name.

"Chassidy."

"Right. You've never even mentioned *Chassidy*." I said with disdain.

"I didn't want to hurt Tamika."

"Well, how did she find out about her?"

"She saw us together at the library. We were just studying, but when I saw Mika last Wednesday she asked about her. I told her the truth. Chassidy and I have gone on a few dates. We're getting to know each other. Tamika was mad. Things got a little heated, and the next thing I knew she was telling me she loved me."

"So you don't really know this Chassidy girl."

"Kelly, I love music. That's simple and easy. But, Chassidy... Chassidy has me confused. I never thought I would get mixed up in this way."

"That makes two of us."

"Duane and Matthew are giving me so much shit over this."

"I'm sure they are. They're probably jealous."

"I wouldn't say that. She won't let me get close to her."

"She's holding out on you? How long have you been talking to Chassidy?" Her name barely rolled off my tongue. Naturally, I disliked her. Witch. She'd worked some type of magic on *Tamika's* DJ.

"Three weeks."

"Three weeks," I shook my head. "Three weeks and who's giving you shit? Wasn't Duane a virgin just last week?" Something told me that it'd been over a week for Duane. He probably lost it the day after we stopped talking, and that's giving him a lot of credit.

"I know, I know. I can wait. I'm just not used to this. I can't even get a kiss."

"Give her time," I pleaded. How quickly I'd forgotten that I wasn't on her side. I was on Tamika's side. But seeing DJ so excited about a girl made me excited. This meant that there was hope for every guy out there like DJ, the guy who refuses to fall in love. But it also meant that there wasn't much hope for every girl like Tamika, the girl who loves the guy who won't commit.

And then there were girls like me. I'd been waiting for Mr. Right, wishing for him, pleading for him. How unfair was it that this perfect girl had just fallen onto DJ's lap when it wasn't even something he was looking for. I chalked it up as just part of the game.

After DJ left, I found myself thinking about Kevin instead of the economics test I had the next day. I'd tossed him aside for the charade I played into with Darius. I wondered if he'd even noticed I left the party early. I considered calling him, but I didn't.

I didn't want to end up in the same type of scenario with Kevin that I'd been in with Darius. So I was relieved when Kevin called me a few days later.

I'd been stuck in my thoughts for the bulk of that week. I'd received a D on my economics test and an incomplete on my humanities paper. It was a little hard to believe that I was generally a 4.0 student. Kevin's call was a welcome distraction from my failure. When he suggested that we have dinner Friday night, I was instantly pulled out of my funk. Tamika couldn't deny that this would be a real date. He was really going to pick me up, and we were really going to eat... together... in a restaurant that didn't have a value menu.

When Kevin called to say that he was on his way, the butterflies kicked in. But they didn't last long. I felt comfortable around Kevin. I was even more comfortable after hearing that he'd faked being bad at calculus just to have an excuse to spend some time with me.

"Why didn't you just ask me out? Don't you see the way girls look at you? Any girl in her right mind would say yes."

"I didn't want to hear *you* say no." He knew the perfect things to say, and I remained in awe as we sat in the understated steakhouse. We made eyes over our menus as we decided what to order. We only made conversation after the server brought our drinks. That's when I realized that Kevin and I really didn't have much in common.

I thoroughly enjoyed reading. He hadn't picked up a book for leisure since elementary school. I liked going to the movies. He said he could never stay awake. I had R&B on my iPod. He only listened to rap. I loved Italian food. He preferred Chinese. I liked the east coast. He wanted to move out west.

But he was fine and charismatic. So I did my best to find a connection.

"I have the cutest pit bull back at my parent's house. But she's more of a terror than my little brother. Do you have any pets?"

"I'm allergic to dogs," he said. "I have a cat though. Jinks. He's as fat as they come. Lazy too. But he's a part of the family." I laughed, but more so at the fact that I hated cats than at his description of Jinks.

"Any siblings?" I was determined to find something, anything, we had in common.

"Nope, it's just me. My parents had me young and split up when I was two. Neither of them remarried, and neither of them have any other kids."

"So which of them raised you? Mom or dad?"

"Dad. He's as military as they come. I grew up making a perfect bed at 0600 hours every day. But he's alright."

"My parents are still together. I've always been a daddy's girl, but I've recently grown close to my mom."

"Me too," he said. Finally, I'd found it. "My mom's easier to talk to. She's mild mannered. My dad's high strung." Nope. Our parents sounded nothing alike.

Kevin and I weren't opposites in the same way that Tayo and I were. I thought about it as we walked back to the car. There was an invisible string that connected me to Tayo. I wasn't sure I'd find that with Kevin.

My uncertainty made me wonder whether or not I'd give him a goodnight kiss. I wasn't one to decide pre-date whether or not I'd allow a guy a goodnight kiss. If it felt right, it was a go. If not, maybe next time. But now that we were on our way home, the decision was right in front of me. To kiss or not to kiss? I would never be the one to initiate it. But if I lingered while making direct eye contact before we parted, I was asking for it. And I was pretty sure that Kevin would succumb.

The first kiss always felt like a chore. You just never knew what you'd get out of it. Very rarely did fireworks go off. Most men were mediocre kissers. And since most would rather bang than kiss, I gave them the benefit of the doubt by assuming that they hadn't had enough practice.

I looked forward to the second kiss. When you already knew what you were getting yourself into. But since I was on the fence about Kevin, needing something to push me one way or the other, I decided to give the first a go.

The ride home was a quiet one, but soon enough we approached my dorm room. I stopped a few feet short of it and turned toward Kevin. "Thank you. For the food and the company," I said.

"Well I'm hoping we can do it again sometime."

"Me too."

"Yeah?" He stepped toward me.

"Yep." I made eye contact.

"I'll definitely be in touch." He slowly pulled me in.

And then it happened. His lips met mine in a kiss that would go down in history. It was one for the movies. It was the kiss that every woman must experience to know the definition of a kiss because that kiss was the worst of my life – a veritable guide on everything not to do. It was all wrong, from the texture of his lips to the taste of his tongue.

There wasn't really anywhere to go from a bad kiss. Maybe I would've given him a second chance if there'd been more chemistry on the date. Another one bites the dust. Or maybe I bit it.

Really, Kevin was just another guy who I'd quickly fallen for and just as quickly found disappointing. I could sulk about it or I could go out with the guys who *never* disappointed me. I thought they might find a little humor in my night. They always did when I told them about my dates.

So I made plans to get drinks with DJ and Matthew. Brianna had a new job at a bar not too far from campus, and we were long overdue for a visit. When DJ picked me up in his champagne colored Acura, I was a little surprised to see a girl in the front seat. She opened the door of the coupe and pushed up the seat to let me in the back. Who was this girl and what made her think that she was a shoe-in for shotgun?

"Hey, I'm Kelly," I said before stepping in.

"Hi. Chassidy."

Chassidy? What made DJ think I would be cool with this? He knew better. I squeezed into the backseat and slid in behind the driver's seat. That way, I'd be able to keep an eye on her. My discomfort with her presence hadn't quenched my curiosity.

Chassidy was brown-skinned and much smaller than me. When she'd stepped out of the car, I'd easily noticed the inches I had on her. And the weight as well. I was thin, but at least ten pounds heavier than she. I noticed how well her dainty voice fit her stature as she talked to DJ.

"Where are we going again?" she asked. I instantly took her for a nagger. It gave me a solid reason to dislike her beyond loyalty to Tamika.

"Bar Ten," he answered. "We'll be there in five."

"Hey, Deej," I squealed. I put my arm around the seat to give his shoulder a hard squeeze.

"What's up?" he managed after a cringe.

"You didn't tell me we were bringing friends." I turned to look at Chassidy. As she turned to face me, a small smile slid across her face and I noticed her dimples. They were as deep and attractive as DJ's. I have to admit that she had a very cute face, girlish and refined.

"I didn't think it would matter," he answered.

"Oh, it doesn't," I assured him. "I did have a story to share with you. About Kevin. But it can wait. The more, the merrier."

"Good," Chassidy piped in. "Because I kind of invited myself. I wouldn't want DJ to get in trouble for my intrusiveness." She'd picked the perfect word. She was, after all, an intruder.

"What are you studying, Chassidy?" I asked.

"Communications. Legal comm major, Spanish minor." I didn't recognize her as a fellow communications student, but she was a couple of years younger. I remembered DJ saying that she was a sophomore.

"I'm communications too. Advertising major."

"Yeah, I've seen you around. I went to an American Advertising Federation meeting. You're on the board, right?"

"Yeah, I am. PR chair."

"Right. I remember," she said. I was a little flattered by her recognition. There was always that simple camaraderie between students in the same field, but I still didn't like her. I was determined not to.

We circled the block Bar Ten was on three times before a parking spot opened up. After spotting Matthew waiting in his car, we all walked in together. We instantly saw Brianna leaning on the bar, flirting with a customer. Typical Brianna. When she caught sight of us, she completely ignored the flirting man in front of her and ran to meet us.

"Kelly! You didn't tell me you were coming."

"Yes I did."

"Well, you know I have the worst memory," she said. "Who are you?" she said bluntly when she saw an unfamiliar face with the group.

"Chassidy," DJ answered for the smiling girl beside him.

"Well, I'm Brianna. Where's Mika?" I realized Brianna had no idea what was going on with DJ and Tamika.

"She couldn't come. Lacrosse practice," I answered curtly.

"Oh. Well, sit down. What are we drinking?"

What I thought would be a completely awkward outing, wasn't. Chassidy was pretty entertaining. She wasn't shy in the least bit. She was the type of person who always drove the conversation to something inappropriate. She was also the type who could knot the stem of her cherry with her tongue, and she didn't hesitate to show us. She told us stories about her obscene family. And she had jokes. Like real "Two guys walk into a bar…" jokes. Getting drinks with her wasn't so bad, I shamefully admitted to myself.

A couple of days later she sent me a request to be her Facebook friend. It was just like a girl to want to get in good with her potential boyfriend's female friends. But I had to admit that I didn't dislike Chassidy. She wasn't the sharpest tool in the shed or the most thoughtful, but I had no intentions of becoming close to a good-time girl. She was only tolerable and fun to have around at a party or a bar.

Before I got the chance to have too many good times with Chassidy, I realized that she was having an effect on my relationship with DJ, and not a positive one. As quickly as DJ had fallen for the girl, I was losing touch with him. I couldn't call him at any hour, and he always brought her when *we* made plans to go out for drinks. I missed hearing his rants about Tamika, which, I guess I should've realized, stopped a long time ago. I didn't want a new female best friend. I wanted my old male best friend. I needed my crutch back.

But that's what happens to coed friendships, isn't it? They disintegrate when a real significant other weasels her way in. That number they put on speed dial changes, and suddenly you've been replaced. She's entitled to shotgun, free drinks and his secrets. Because of the tumultuous nature of DJ's relationship with Tamika, there'd always been space for me. But his new relationship with Chassidy told me I was being replaced, and I had no choice but to sit back and watch it happen. Shallow witch.

Desperate to hang onto our friendship, I surprised DJ, knocking on his door when I knew Chassidy had class.

"What story did you have about Kevin? First date?" he asked after I arrived.

"Yeah. We had nothing in common. But the worst of it was the goodnight kiss."

"Sloppy?" he asked with raised eyebrows.

"I wouldn't say sloppy. Just not good, I guess." I scrunched my nose and shook my head.

"So is he done?"

"Yeah. I'm over it. And right before Valentine's Day too. Great." I threw up my hands in surrender. "I don't know why I can't seem to make it work with any of these guys. I must have been cursed as a kid or something."

"Nah, you'll find him. Just gotta be patient."

"Yep, you're probably right, dad." DJ hated it when I called him dad. So I continued to do it. He sighed, unaffected by my jab.

"So, let's hear what you've been working on."

DJ wasn't just a DJ. He produced music too. And every now and then, I'd write over his music. Sometimes his beats sounded just like his personality. Friendly and cool. But every now and then, he'd throw me a song so foreign to his character that I hardly believed he produced it. Those were the songs that mesmerized me.

"How did you come up with this?" I'd ask.

"I don't know. It's a feeling."

"I want to get feelings," I joked.

"You have more feelings than just about anyone I know."

"So you think I could be a DJ, a producer?" I asked.

"Nah," he laughed. "But I think you could be... something."

"Oh gee, thank you," I responded dramatically.

But honestly, what did DJ have that I didn't? What was I missing? I considered myself a creative being.

"What did you write?" he changed the subject.

I read him the chorus.

Can't we live tonight (baby, baby)
I don't wanna be right (baby, baby)
Wings unspent and I'm just flying
Shoot me down, no just stop trying
Can't we live tonight

I've never really been a lyricist. I crumpled my paper and threw it at him. He caught it.

"Why did you write this? I mean, what made you write these words?"

"I don't know."

"I think you had a feeling!"

"Maybe."

"I think you're a writer." Moments like those were what drew me to DJ. He'd unintentionally given me hope for more. It wasn't the hope that my girlfriends gave me in men. It was something else. It was the same hope he had for his music. Somehow he managed to maintain his love for music all the while falling for Chassidy. I guess I'd underestimated the capacity of the human heart. He could probably maintain his love for his female best friend too. And I was thankful for that.

For the next week, I couldn't get those words out of my head. "I think you're a writer." It was nothing new to me. I'd always been a writer. I just never knew *what* to write. Lyrics weren't it.

CHAPTER SEVEN: MR. SECOND BEST

Some say that first place is the only place that matters.

I didn't hate Valentine's Day. Sure, it reminded the single that we were, in fact, single. But what day in the middle of winter didn't? Valentine's Day was truly only horrible when you'd just started dating someone new. It was hard to decide what was too much and what was not enough.

Say you'd gone on two dates with a guy and he conveniently forgot V-Day. Deal breaker. There was just nothing worse than a man who denied the existence of the obnoxiously pink and red holiday. And even worse was the excuse, "I don't celebrate Hallmark holidays." Well, I did. And just to put it out there, most women did.

I had never been too keen on the idea of spending the day with my girls like some single women did either. Though they were loved, bridesmaids would never replace a groom, and I didn't like the idea of pretending that they did.

So I spent my last college Valentine's Day alone. It would be the first time in my four-year tenure that I wasn't asked out. It felt as if no man, other than my father, even acknowledged me that day.

My father always sent my sister and me chocolates that arrived on Valentine's Day, not a day after or a day before. He believed that every girl deserved a reminder that they were loved on this day. Since he could never be sure if Cupid had stepped in for us each year, he took it upon himself to ensure we got a little something to celebrate the day. As I ate my chocolates alone, I thought about my first college Valentine's Day and the one I'd let get away. I couldn't help but wonder why some people got to stay friends after they'd been romantically involved while others didn't.

My odd, undefined entanglement with Darius triggered some new, unwanted experiences for me after I resorted to ignoring him. It was partly because of my first college valentine, Ben.

I didn't figure it out until our second date, the end of our second date to be exact. Ben had taken me to Baltimore because I mentioned on our first date that I'd never been.

Baltimore wasn't the most glamorous city, but at night the harbor shone bright, and I was happy that Ben decided to make the long drive there. He was one of the few freshmen who had a car. When I was with him, I thought of all the places that he could take me, and not just in that car of his. Ben was going places.

He was a business student and a productive one at that. At nineteen, he already had his own business up and running. Yep, he was *that* college student.

I met him in my German class. I'd been taking German since elementary school and was fairly good at it. I came to class late, left early, completed the homework in minutes and still managed to ace all of the tests and quizzes. Ben was half German, making him the closest I'd ever come to dating a white guy. He was impressed with my ability to outsmart him in his own language. He was fluent but his reading and writing needed work. He hadn't learned the language in a formal environment like I had.

He asked me out in the cafeteria while I was sitting with Casey. He and his friend assertively approached our table.

"Hi. I'm Ben. We have German together. This is my friend Daniel. Can we sit with you?"

"Sure," I answered. We'd spoken a few times in class. "I'm Kelly. This is Casey."

"Hey," Casey smiled. Daniel hadn't spoken. I could tell that he was probably on the shy side, coerced into sitting with us by his friend. But Ben didn't make him sit for long. He got right to the point.

"I was wondering if you wanted to go out sometime." It wasn't really rocket science. Ben was smart, and bold. He'd taken a chance in asking me out in front of his friend and mine. Not to mention, he was easy on the eyes. He had very bright, light brown skin with one of those perfectly placed moles.

"Umm, sure," I said nonchalantly even though I was beyond flattered.

"I'll just take down your number then." He pulled out his cell phone, and I recited my number. "Well, we gotta go. Enjoy your lunch, ladies."

He was all that we could talk about after he left. He was some type of smooth. It's no wonder a whole group of girls started hating on me for dating him. They said that I stole him from their friend Jamie. But if I was a thief, it was one of the most effortless burglaries to date. Ben did all of the work.

The restaurant he took me to in Baltimore was just as impressive as the city's lights. As we neared the end of our meal, he asked me if I'd dated anyone else at Davis. I simply told him, "There was a guy. It turned out he had a girlfriend so I let him go."

"Yeah, I know about Darius," Ben said. I was taken aback by this confession. "A few of us had a conversation about dating girls who your boys have already dated. With guys it's a free for all until someone takes her out. After that though, it's bad business. Dirty money, you know. But in our case, Darius had a girlfriend so he has no claim. He and I aren't all that close anyway."

"Close enough to discuss me," I said in awe. "I didn't even know that you guys knew each other."

"Well, we have a few mutual friends. He's a cool guy. I don't have anything against him. Do you?"

"No," I laughed. "But, I don't see us being friends anytime soon."

"I wouldn't force that on you," he smiled. "Are you over him?" With that question, I was pretty much over talking about Darius, but I understood his curiosity so I answered.

"Yeah. I'm here with you, aren't I?" It wasn't a completely honest answer, but I couldn't say I'm here with you because I'm trying to get over him. He was too great of a guy to slap in the face in public over a plate of shrimp scampi.

I'd never been on a date with the friend of a former crush. Now I understood Ben's insistence that we go to Baltimore. He wanted to be the first to take me. I guess he wanted to be the first in any capacity. Though I stress, Darius and I never technically dated.

For some reason he liked me a lot, much more than his friends wanted him to. After hearing about Darius, they were all against me. Somehow Darius had portrayed me as the bad guy and they all bought into it. Well, all of them except for Ben.

All I did was start dating a nice guy, and I had groups of girls and guys rallying against me. Again, I'd never been that girl before.

I'd also never been the girl that had two valentines on Valentine's Day. But that February, I became that girl. Ben asked me to be his valentine first. I was hesitant in accepting the title because I wasn't sure what it entailed. First I was his valentine, and then I was what? His girlfriend? I definitely wasn't ready to be that. So I was upfront with my questions.

"What is a valentine anyway?" I asked him.

"It just means that you're my girl for the day," he answered simply.

"Well, ok. But we have to do things my way. I don't want to go to dinner."

"I have class Wednesday night. So, it would've been an awfully late dinner anyway. What do you have in mind?"

"My choice. My dorm room. 9:30 sharp. I'll surprise you."

It seemed like the perfect Valentine's Day, and it probably would've been had Danielle not intervened in my plans. Valentine's Day morning, she asked me for a favor.

"You remember Branden's friend, Camren, right? Tall. Dark. Handsome."

"Yeah, he was nice. What about him?" I couldn't tell where the conversation was headed. Unknowingly, I began making my bed. Danielle stood in our full-length mirror grooming herself.

"Well, Branden sorta asked me if we could double for Valentine's Day and I sorta told him... yes."

"We as in... me and Camren? You and Branden?"

"Yeah."

"What about Ben? Wouldn't you say three's a crowd?" I regained my composure.

"Just yesterday you said that Ben has class. You'll be back before he gets out. Please, Kelly. I really want to go and Branden doesn't want to leave Camren out. He says Cam's been in a funk since his high school sweetheart broke up with him a few weeks ago."

"So you're bringing me along to babysit?" I nearly shouted as I found myself facing her. With her books in hand, she was all set to go to class. She'd be late if I didn't give her a quick yes or no.

"No," I shook my head.

"Kelly," she pouted. "Please."

"Ugh," I groaned. "But we have to be back by eight. And let's try to go somewhere low-key, please."

At the time, I didn't really know what I'd done. Ben's class ended at nine so I couldn't foresee any nicks in the plan. If all went well, I'd be back with plenty of time to spare.

I set everything up before I went on the double date. I'd purchased some dessert for us and borrowed pillows from all of my friends. My side of the room was plush enough to break a man's forty-foot fall.

Dinner wasn't so bad. Camren wasn't interested in me, and I wasn't interested in him. That much was clear. But the company was nice. Branden and Danielle were nothing short of adorable. It was the start of a long relationship between the two of them. She really owed me one, especially since we completely lost track of time and I found myself practically running to get back to campus. By the time I reached the front doors of Booker Hall, it was nearing ten o'clock.

Ben hadn't called, and I didn't see him in the lobby. There was the possibility that he was running late as well. Maybe something had kept him after class, I hoped as I raced to my room. But as I turned the corner I saw him sitting with his legs stretched out and crossed in front of my door. He'd been using his phone for entertainment, and there was some sort of a goodie bag beside him. If he was mad, I couldn't tell. He just looked tired.

"How long have you been here?" I asked.

"Thirty minutes."

"I'm really sorry. My roommate Danielle begged me to go out with her and some friends. I thought I'd be back in time. Who checked you into the dorm?" Ben lived in the all-boys dorm a few blocks away. He must have had some other Booker Hall resident check him in.

"I ran into Darius on my way in. And again about ten minutes ago on his way to the computer lab. It was kind of awkward with me out here still waiting for you." His friends had warned him about me and I was proving them right.

"I feel awful. Do you still want to come in?"

"I'll still take my surprise," he said with a smile. He handed me the bag. Inside, there was a teddy bear with a folded note hanging from his neck. I removed the ribbon and unfolded the note.

"Can't even wait until we get inside?"
"Nope," I grinned.
The note read:

> *In case there is any confusion...*
> *Val-en-tine:*
> 1. *"A sweetheart chosen or complimented on Valentine's Day."*
> 2. *"A gift or greeting sent or given especially to a sweetheart on Valentine's Day... expressing uncritical praise or affection."*
> With uncritical praise and affection,
> Ben

It was all that I'd ever wanted in a card. Short, sweet, and to the point. He hadn't overdone it. It was just enough to make me smile.

"Thank you, Ben," I said as I hugged him. "I guess we can go in now."

"What's up with all of the pillows?" he asked once inside.

"It's called a pillow party," I said. "I've created a playlist of some of my favorite songs. Get comfortable. We're lounging out to some great music and with an assortment of desserts."

"What have you got over there?" He'd taken a seat on a few of the pillows and was watching me unwrap the desserts.

"Carrot cake. Cheesecake. Pound cake. Cookies. Brownies. Blondies. Chocolate covered strawberries. And I got my friend to buy a bottle of champagne." I was only nineteen at the time.

"The works," he said. "Who's going to eat all of this?"

I shrugged. "All of the choices are what makes it so much fun. My mom introduced me to pillow parties when I was younger. Anytime Karol or I was upset we had one. We'd eat our favorite desserts and dance around the room to our favorite songs until whoever the downer was cheered up. That's how you work off the dessert, of course, by dancing."

"You're going to make me dance?"

"You don't have to," I shook my head. "I figured we could just talk."

The night was wrong. I don't mean to say that it was a bad night. We had a fun time and enjoyed each other's company. But it wasn't right, and I knew that from the first song – "For The Love Of You." The Isley Brothers sang about not wanting to be anywhere but with their love.

Truth is, there was some place I'd rather be. And someone

who I'd rather be with. But instead I was here with one of his friends. *When had I become that girl?*

Ben had never heard most of the songs I played and wasn't a big fan of the ones that he did recognize. He didn't say it, but I could tell. When a song really registers with someone, it's impossible to hide.

"You don't like this music?" I asked.

"It's not that I don't like it. I just don't know it. I just have to get used to it." Much like romance, music doesn't work that way. At least I didn't think so then.

We did dance that night. We slow danced. Just for one song. It only took that one slow dance. I wouldn't allow myself to get too close to him, and it was something that he could sense.

As he left that night he gave me a hard hug. "I'll be in touch," he said.

"Ben, I don't think I'm ready –"

"I know," he cut me off.

The relationship had barely started before we broke up on Valentine's Day. A few weeks later, I apologized to Darius. I apologized for ignoring him, but I never mentioned Ben. I didn't see the need to drag Ben through anymore mud. Darius coldly accepted the apology as if he was never hurt, but I know that he was.

To some extent I'd hurt Darius Monroe. When a woman hurts a man he'll spend the next three years pouting about it. Then, apparently, the woman will ask him out at a friend's birthday party but won't stick around to hear his answer because, unlike her, he never apologized. He should've apologized for hurting her, for having a girlfriend and for causing her to let a damned good guy turn into the one that got away. She'd let him get away because he was second best to someone she hadn't been able to get closure with.

CHAPTER EIGHT: THE QUESTION MARK

*Could love realistically be 100 percent romance?
Maybe it was whatever we believed it to be.*

A couple of weeks after my horrible kiss with Kevin, I found my world spinning. My life was starting to spiral out of control, or at least that's how *he* made me feel. He was a new guy who unexpectedly dropped into the picture. I once read that love was like a black hole that some people chose to fall into and others, the smart ones, walked around. It was too early to tell if I had fallen into some bottomless hole, but I did know that I was on shaky ground.

Most of the time I could tell you exactly why I was dating a guy. He dressed well. He was smart. He had a perfect set of teeth. He made me laugh. It didn't take me long to realize that the one to be afraid of was the one I couldn't fit into a box.

We met at a movie pre-screening hosted by my internship. At five-foot-five and weighing in at a buck fifteen, I was inexplicably given the task of bouncer at the event. I had to man the door and ensure people's names were on the list and they were at least eighteen, or turn them away. His name wasn't on the list, but his best friend's was, plus one. When they approached me, I had to admit that I was a bit nervous. His name was Malcolm.

"Yours?" he asked after I checked his ID and recorded his name on the plus one list.

"I'm Kelly."

"You're the woman in charge here, huh?"

"I wish," I said with a laugh. "I'm just an intern. Hence the remedial task of matching names to ID."

"You'll get there though. I can tell. You have that intelligent, ambitious look about you." If I were a little bit lighter, my cheeks would have been rosy red.

"Are you a journalist?" I asked, indicating the pen and pad he had in hand.

"No, I'm a film student at the University of Maryland."

"Oh. Well, I hope you enjoy the film."

"I hope so too. You're not going to miss it, are you?"

"Probably, actually. But I'll catch it when it hits the theater."

"You can take me to see it. How about that?" He lifted his eyebrows and hands together in question.

"*Me* take *you*?" I asked.

"Well, yeah. Like I said, you look like a woman in charge." For the first time, I looked at him. I really looked at him. I looked at him the way you look at someone you're trying to paint – not only taking in every distinct feature and minor detail of his person but also trying to find the inside from the outside.

He was about six feet of dark chocolate with dark brown eyes that constantly twinkled. His face was cleanly shaven except for the trace of hair along his chin. His full lips looked like they'd constantly been bitten, explaining their raw red tint.

"Can I get your number?" he asked.

"Umm, well, you can give me yours." I didn't want any of my fellow interns, or better yet my boss, seeing me handing out my number. Malcolm quickly scribbled his number on the pad he'd brought with him, tore out the sheet and handed it to me.

"See, you are in charge," he said. "Call me if you want to have a good time." He caught up with his friend who was waiting a few feet ahead. "But only if you want to have a good time," he called back.

I hadn't intended to call. I probably shouldn't have. But I did. I called – probably because somewhere in the back of my mind, lights flashed the words, "the one."

So I dialed the possibility. But what do you say to the guy who passed you his number while you were at work? I decided to play into his pick-up line.

"So, how do you plan on showing me a good time?"

"To be honest, I didn't have any particular plans in mind, but I'm a fun guy and you seem like a girl who could use some fun. You looked a bit stressed out at the premiere."

"Well, I hate my internship."

"And why is that?"

"For starters, they give me tedious, remedial busy work. And then there's my prick of a boss. She can't count to two without using her fingers. I should just quit. I'll probably be working at Neon Advertising after graduation anyway."

He laughed. I thought he'd chime in and offer a similar experience or tell me to hang in there. But instead he said, "You know what I decided this year? I decided that I am going to be unconditionally happy. It's all a state of mind, you know? Happiness, fear, sadness, self-loathing, contentment."

"Are you saying that I choose not to be happy with my internship?"

"Well, when I saw you the other night, I knew I had to speak to you. I thought, there she is. Gorgeous skin, perfectly tailored outfit, not a strand of hair out of place. The only thing missing was your smile. And whether or not you realize it, we choose to smile. Or in your case, not to."

"You do know that I'm not some unhappy girl waiting on a knight in shining armor?" Hmm, well at least the "unhappy" part of that statement was true.

"No, I know you're not waiting to be rescued, which is a good thing. Besides, I'm not here to rescue you."

"Then what are you here for?"

"I'm here to see you smile." The line seemed a bit corny to me, and it was the first of many that would make me dubious of his character. What were his intentions? How honest was all of this flattery? Was he being truthful or was it all rehearsed and used many times before?

In between the corny lines, I learned a lot about Malcolm that night. He had a mother, a grandma and two older sisters. They were all exceptionally strong women, the ones who would never succumb to peer pressure. They went against the grain, never compromising or conceding their point. And they embraced their natural beauty, something that seemed to be a real challenge for black women in America. He loved them, adored them even. I found my confidence wavering as I wondered what he saw in me.

Maybe he liked how stubborn and decided I was. Things are never grey in my world. They're black or white. Michael Jackson definitely bleached his skin. Women should absolutely never wear white tights. Spitting in public is rude and disgusting. My friend Sarah, who occasionally switches teams, well, she is gay –

no question.

Maybe he liked my aspirations. For a while we discussed advertising. He said he liked the pitch in my voice when I talked about it, more elated than my normal octave.

Whatever it was he saw, whatever it was that caused such flattery worked wonders on me. I became super girly, full of emotion and giggles, batting my eyes and curling my hair. Malcolm. I liked that name. I said it over and over in my head. I couldn't wait for our first date.

We went to the movies to see *Basic Behavior*, the same movie he'd seen at the screening. I thought the date would be explosive. It had to be. I was already so into him. But after the movie, as we sat at a late-night diner across the street from the theater, waiting on our over-cooked chicken fingers and perfectly salted fries, I took note that he was a little awkward and began to reassess previous thoughts about him being the one.

That feeling of uncertainty remained as he walked me to my dorm. We were discussing our favorite movies. Many of mine, he had never seen, which I thought a little odd for a film student though his interest was in documentaries.

"How have you never seen *Love Jones*? It's the movie of all movies, the epitome of black love."

He shrugged.

"*Mo' Better Blues*?"

"Nope."

"But that's classic Spike Lee."

He shook his head.

"Ok. Ok. *Poetic Justice*?"

"Umm, no."

"And you call yourself a film student? We have to watch *Love Jones*. Like tonight. Right now."

And so we did. We watched the movie that made me fall in love with Larenz Tate and want to be Nia Long. But watching it with Malcolm was probably not the best idea. All of those romantic feelings I had for the movie spilled onto him like splattered paint. Not too long after, I found myself spinning.

Our relationship grew quickly from there. Every day at around lunchtime, he'd text me. You know, your typical, "how is your day?" or "just thinking about you." When we talked on the phone, it was easy to hear just how much he adored me. He liked the sound of my voice. He got my humor, which could be a bit biting at times. He loved that I loved advertising. He respected my opinion, even if it differed from his. If I was spinning, then he was... he was... in love?

A week later, we decided to spend our Saturday night in. *Mo' Better Blues* was on the menu – part two of his introduction to black cinematography. This time we went to his place.

Malcolm's place didn't look like your typical college apartment. College students' living rooms usually had a mismatched arrangement of the bare necessities – a TV, couch and a randomly placed chair or two. The place that Malcolm shared with his two best friends was fully decorated. Their living room held a black leather sofa and matching love seat. Their TV sat on a fully stocked bookshelf. They'd littered the walls with black art. Apparently, a friend of theirs was a very talented artist.

As we made our way to the kitchen, the buttery smell of baking cornbread filled the air. We found his two roommates there, one behind the stove and the other at their small dining room table. Malcolm told me earlier that we'd be having dinner in. Phil, the one behind the stove, liked to cook, and everyone had taken to calling him Chef.

I'd be hesitant to let a female friend of mine cook for my man, and I wouldn't dare let her cook before he and I defined the relationship. Technically, this was only our second date. Don't they say that the way to a man's heart is through his stomach? Well, I believe that to be true for mankind in general so I couldn't say I didn't give Chef a second glance.

I'd always envisioned myself with a man who could cook. My friends criticized me for seeking that in a man when I, myself, didn't cook. I always told them that the day I met that man, the one, would be the day I make myself comfortable in the kitchen. Until then, no one cooked for my dates.

Malcolm's other roommate, Lenny, was playing music on his laptop. Ask anyone in that house and he'd say that Lenny was the next big thing. I had to admit that I liked his music. It was a unique combination of sound that was like a mixture of Kanye West and old school Slick Rick.

He barely turned down the music as we made our plates in preparation to eat. It was just low enough for us to hear each other. I let Malcolm lead me through the food line. As I held my plate, he scooped a large portion for himself and a smaller portion for me. Our plates filled with grilled chicken, sautéed vegetables, potato salad and cornbread. Chef had outdone himself.

I was a little surprised when we all sat at the table. I expected

Phil and Lenny to sit in front of the TV, leaving the table for just the two of us. Then I realized that I was guest starring in their family dinner. Was I meeting the parents, or was I one of the boys?

Chef and Malcolm did most of the talking at first. I got the feeling that Lenny wasn't much of a talker. Maybe he saved it for his music. Nerves kept me quiet. I didn't really know what to say to this family of men.

"How do you like it, Kelly?" Phil asked from across the table.

"It's really good. Thank you for cooking. Tell me you're not the only one who cooks around here." I shot Malcolm a playful glance.

"He moonlights behind the stove every now and then," Phil said in an effort to save his friend.

"You cook, Kelly?" Malcolm asked.

"You got me there." The table laughed. "But I'm not against learning. Chef, you'll have to teach me a thing or two." Oh no, was I flirting with him? If I was, Malcolm didn't seem to mind.

"He can. I've been gaining weight ever since we moved into this place."

"That makes two of us," Lenny added.

Malcolm's phone rang and he excused himself to take the call. If things were awkward before, they were even more so now. But Chef didn't seem to think so. He kept the questions coming.

"What are you studying at Davis?"

"Advertising. I want to work in creative services. Probably as a copywriter."

"Hmm. I don't think I know any other advertisers. That's pretty cool. Can I see some of your work?" First he was cooking for me. Now he wanted to see my advertising portfolio. Who was I dating here again?

"I didn't bring anything with me. I'll make sure to next time."

"I look forward to it."

Chef and I got to talking, and the situation started to become a little less awkward for me. He shared some of his best cooking tips, and even told me about the first time that he cooked with his mother. He was the oldest of four. Helping his mother cook for his younger siblings brought the two of them together every night. They were still extremely close. The conversation was flowing easily but soon fifteen minutes had passed without Malcolm returning. Chef went to find out what was holding him up.

Lenny and I silently sat alone. He'd finished his plate and gone back to the same position he was in when I'd met him, his head less than a foot away from his computer. I nibbled on a small piece of cornbread. A minute later, Malcolm and Chef laughed their way back to the table.

"You don't just leave your date at the dinner table," I heard Chef say.

"I had to take it. It was about the video Sergio is editing."

"Rude nonetheless."

"I'm sorry, Kelly," Malcolm said, reclaiming his seat beside me. "And look, you've already finished."

"It's ok. Take your time." I understood group projects so I let it slide. I forced myself to overlook the fact that Malcolm had not only let Chef cook for me, but he'd also let him eat with me. Almost alone. What type of swingers' house was this?

When Malcolm and I were finally left alone, we popped in *Mo' Better Blues*. We sat shoulder to shoulder on the loveseat directly in front of their 42-inch television.

"This better be good, Kelly."

"Relax. It is. I promise."

"You owe me dinner, homemade, if it isn't."

"And you owe me if it is. Bet?"

"Let's kiss on it." Malcolm pulled me in, but I held my head at a distance.

"Too soon," I said and patted his knee. "Watch the movie. I don't want you to miss anything."

He promptly backed off and didn't try to pressure me. I felt comfortable with Malcolm, with his arm around me. At 6'1", he was the perfect height. I fell into the nook of his neck and if I turned my head to the side, I'd effortlessly find the perfect place to nuzzle. In other words, we were geometrically sound. And I was attracted to him. His head was well shaped, which I found to be an underrated and often rare quality in a man. Even after middle age, when men go bald, Malcolm would still look great.

I watched him watch the movie. I waited for him to smile during the intimate scenes and laugh at the comedic moments. I couldn't help but talk him through my favorite parts.

"So, what did you think?" I asked as the credits rolled.

"I liked it a lot for a romance."

"Do you believe that they were in love? Pure love? 100 percent romantic love?"

"Of course. Don't you?" he responded.

"I used to. But my mother made me think twice about it. She suggested that their love, like all love, is often equal parts romance and circumstance."

"Love should be all romance. At least that's what I'm expecting."

I didn't love the movie any less, but my mother's suggestion had put a spin on it in my mind. It slipped out of the romance category. She'd made it too real for that category. My mother had a way of doing that.

I always found myself teetering the line of reality and romance, never completely sure of what I believed or how I felt. I was looking for "the one" but not sure that I'd ever find him. Malcolm's certainty made me smile. He certainly believed in romance. And I certainly liked that about him.

"So, when's dinner?" I said with a smile, having won the bet.

"You're really not going to let me off the hook?"

"Nope. I want dinner. What are you cooking?"

"I'll surprise you sometime next week."

"Alright. I like surprises."

"Want to watch another movie? Or just some TV? It's not too late yet. I can take you home after."

"Let's watch TV. Where's the remote?"

At the same time, we both spotted the remote on the bookshelf beside the DVD player.

"You're closer," he said, laughing.

"I'm too tired to get up. Can you?" I pleaded.

"But you're closer." He sounded like a child.

"Barely." I stubbornly kept my seat. "C'mon, Malcolm."

"Why do I always have to get up?" he whined.

"Always?" I questioned. "This is only our second date."

"Yeah, but I put the DVD in. It wouldn't hurt you to get up and get the remote."

We sat in silence for what seemed like ages but was probably just a minute or two before I gave in because, really, who fights about getting up to get the remote on the second date? I guess I thought getting the remote would be the manly thing for Malcolm to do, but it wasn't worth a fight. Not on the second date.

Malcolm drove me home a little over an hour later. I still hadn't stopped spinning. I was in a whirlpool of him – even though he hadn't cooked, he'd for the most part missed dinner, he'd made me fetch the remote, and he wasn't a Davis man. There was still something about him. I enjoyed being lost in him.

But I questioned him like I questioned the dynamics of love. Was he forever? Was what we had romance? I didn't want my heart broken when his true colors inevitably pierced my obstructed, love-crazed view.

CHAPTER NINE: THE GRADUATE PART II

*Meet new men but keep the old.
Some are silver but the others are gold.*

I had no intentions of spending the night. But in this case, spending the night didn't mean what it typically meant. We moved to his bedroom after his roommates took over the big screen in the living room to watch basketball. We fell asleep watching standup comedy, so we had literally only slept together.

I awoke with my face plastered to one of his shabby red pillows and one arm casually thrown across his chest. I was about to leap up, frustrated that I'd missed the alarm clock I'd never set but remembered that it was Sunday. No class. No work. I'd have to catch church next week. I sighed with relief.

I tiptoed out of bed and checked my phone for messages and missed calls. Two text messages. DJ wanted to know about my plans for the night. Tamika wanted to borrow my new black leggings. There was also a voicemail from an unknown number. I'd recently gotten a new phone and hadn't completed updating my contact list. It could have been from any number of people so I listened to the message.

"Kelly, this is Tayo. We haven't talked in awhile. I'm not sure why. Well, it might be because I'm an insensitive jerk. I'm finding it hard to be vulnerable here. But you should know that I m-i-s-s you. It's much easier to spell than it is to say. Well, bye. Call me back. If you want."

I froze. Tayo's words went straight to my heart, just as they always had.

"Morning," breathed Malcolm.

I turned to face him. As our eyes met, I dropped the phone I loosely held in my right hand. I put Tayo out of my mind as quickly as he'd filled it. I snuggled back into bed with my very own moviemaker. We stayed in that comfortable position for another hour – my arm tight across his chest and his arm around my shoulder. Nothing new. Nothing extraordinary. Just comfortable.

Eventually, we thought it best to be hygienic. He gave me an extra toothbrush, and we brushed our teeth together. I think it's safe to say that you like someone when you enjoy brushing your teeth with him. After all, anything done in the bathroom feels somewhat personal. Malcolm's bathroom was no bigger than a broom closet, but we fit. I didn't mind him in my personal space.

"So, what are we doing today?" he asked.

"Well, here's what I would like to do. I'd like to pig out, couch potato style with you. Sloppy. I mean chili fries, cookies and cream, day old pizza sloppy. But I can't. I've been bombing economics lately, and it's imperative that I get some serious studying done."

"Are you sure? Sloppy sounds like more fun."

"Don't you want me to graduate?"

"Well, when you put it like that, let me know when you're ready to go," he sighed.

Malcolm dropped me off at my dorm a little over an hour later. On my way in, I ran into DJ on his way out.

"Hey, Kelly, where have you been?" he asked with a smirk.

"It was an accident. I fell asleep over Malcolm's."

"Oh, ok."

"Sorry I missed your text last night," I said in an effort to change the subject.

"Oh, no problem."

"What did you end up doing?"

"We went out for Tayo's birthday. I know you guys are off and on, but I thought you might want to come."

"His birthday?" I asked in shock. "I completely forgot. His birthday is... when? It's today, isn't it? Is today the thirtieth?"

"Yep, it's today. How are you guys anyway?"

"I don't know. He called me. We haven't talked in over a month, but he called me last night."

"Maybe he wanted to invite you out with us."

"No, it was too late for an invitation. He called after midnight, and he left a voicemail. Here, take a listen." I watched DJ's eyebrows raise, then lower, then raise again as he listened to the message. He handed me back my phone without commenting. "Well, what do you think?" I prodded him.

"I think you guys go back and forth too much. I can't tell if he's trying to be your friend or something more."

"Exactly," I cosigned. Tayo seemed to like me in his back pocket. He didn't want to be in a relationship, but he wanted me near just in case he changed his mind. He wanted me in hiding but easily within reach for whenever he decided he was ready for me.

Despite knowing this and despite his hurtful colorist mindset, I wasn't free of my feelings for him and for the rhythm we so easily and so often fell back into. Maybe we'd go back and forth until our forties like Carrie Bradshaw and Big. I was left wondering whether I should place him in my back pocket as well.

I gave Tayo a call that night. Just one happy birthday wish.

"Happy birthday. I heard you guys had fun last night."

"Thanks. And we did. I guess DJ told you."

"Yeah. He did. The question is, why didn't you? Why wasn't I invited?"

"I didn't think you'd want to come. Things got so weird last time we hung out. I didn't mean for things to come out the way they did. Your skin is beautiful."

"It's water under the bridge. One day you'll appreciate black women," I joked.

"Well, I already appreciate you," he said. "So, what's new?"

For some reason, no matter how small the possibility, I thought Tayo might express his undying love for me. He didn't. As usual, I was fooled – this time by a voicemail in which Tayo really hadn't said much of anything. He couldn't even say the word "miss."

At the end of our conversation that night, Tayo told me that I shouldn't feel obligated to call him and that he'd leave the ball in my court and wait for me to come around. I thought it just as well. Right after we hung up, I dialed Malcolm. Maybe Tayo was Big, but I wasn't Carrie.

Malcolm and I made plans for the next Friday. By the time it rolled around, I hadn't heard anything else from Tayo. He'd said he wouldn't call, and I knew I wouldn't either. We'd let things go with a friendly goodbye.

As I walked home from class that afternoon, I received a text message from Malcolm. He had to cancel. Or so he said. Something about filming for a project. I wasn't too upset. I was happy to have time to catch up with Tamika and Brianna.

We decided to dress up and go to a club downtown. Brianna went to the club almost every weekend, but Tamika and I usually reserved that experience for special occasions. Rushing to get to the club before they instituted a cover charge just to wait in a line that moved at a snail's speed was hardly our idea of an ideal night. Then, of course, you had to contend with the too dark rooms and the too grabby mean that occupied them. There was also never anywhere to sit unless you wanted to shell out hundreds of dollars for a table. No, Tamika and I did not love the club scene.

But on those rare occasions that we did go to the club, usually to appease Brianna, we made sure to have a good time to make up for the hassles. That particular Friday went especially well because after weeks of sulking about DJ, Tamika met George.

Meeting a guy at the club can be hit-or-miss, but in this case, things looked promising as George was a friend of Marcus. I'd met Marcus after spotting a roach getting too comfortable in my room. Terrified, I ran into the hallway at the very same moment he came humming down the hall, toting a book bag and fast food.

Whoever said it's a man's world was absolutely right. People just fail to realize that it's not because men are physically stronger, and it sure as hell isn't because they're smarter. It's because we live in a world with spiders, roaches, mice and snakes. Where would we be without male help to kill these little demons? Of course I knew there were exceptions to every rule but when it came to this, I was not one of them, which prompted me to ask a complete stranger to enter my room and kill a roach for me.

"Hey. I've seen you around. We haven't met yet. I'm Kelly. And I'm so sorry for this, but I have a favor to ask you."

"Marcus. And uhh… what's up?"

"There's a roach in my room. Can you kill it for me? I really hate bugs." He burst into laughter. Incessant laughter. I almost walked away.

"Sure. Where's he at, babe?" he managed to say. Marcus had that smooth, sweet-talking, gigolo way about him. He regularly used words like "babe" and "sweetheart." He walked tall and carelessly. And drank like a sailor.

George stood awkwardly beside Marcus. He didn't have his finesse. I could tell he was completely sober, unlike my looming friend. There was something calm and kind about George. He wore the face of a gentleman. And I didn't doubt his intelligence solely based on Marcus'.

Marcus introduced the three of us to George. But George only spoke to Tamika. He asked, "How are you, ladies?" But it was clear that he meant, "How are you, Tamika?" And after they got to talking, we went from a threesome to a twosome. Just Brianna and me. Marcus had drunkenly wandered off as the two of us were not satiating his hunger for female attention.

I made it home at around three in the morning. It took everything in me not to drunk dial Malcolm. By the time morning rolled around, I couldn't hold off any longer. When he didn't answer his phone, I decided to send him a text message.

"Maybe I should accidentally fall asleep at your place again tonight." Sent at 10:30 a.m. Chances were he was still asleep so I did not expect an immediate reply. I became worried when the clock struck three in the afternoon and he still hadn't responded. Maybe things weren't going as well as I'd thought.

Malcolm finally called back at around ten that night. He said he was sorry, and that he'd been really busy. I knew that people made time for whom and what they wanted. However, I didn't make the mistake of saying that to Malcolm. I just hoped it wouldn't happen again.

But it did. At least once a week, Malcolm disappeared. I'd call and text in various combination without receiving a reply. His apology was always the same. He was busy. I figured he had to be stick thin. No way he had time to eat. Someone must have told him who won the game last night. No way he had time to watch it. He didn't even have time to say, "I'm busy right now. I'll call you back later." And oddly enough, these super busy days were always on the weekend. At least I had the chance to say that I was dating the busiest man on Earth.

His inattention started off as a phone call at the dinner table, a missed text message and falling asleep on the phone. But it was getting out of hand. My last visit, I'd seen more of Chef than I had of Malcolm. And Chef cooked. Remember that bet Malcolm and I made? The one where he said he would cook for me? Yeah, I was still waiting on that dinner, not that it would live up to a Chef meal. Maybe I was dating the wrong roommate. I found myself thinking of making that switch. At this point, I doubted that Malcolm would even notice if I jumped teams.

This quickly turned us into that bickering couple, the one that made everyone around them uncomfortable. Friends wondered if they should have interfered or just silently witnessed. We bickered like an old married couple, worse than I used to fight with the sister I'd shared a bedroom with through my adolescence.

I didn't think he was giving me enough time. He said I didn't offer him enough affection. Either way, we were off.

Have you ever found yourself in the direct path of a stranger, but instead of going around each other, you danced a bit? You both moved from side to side to clear the path but continued to end up in each other's way. You did this dance until one party was smart enough to remain completely still while the other passed. Let's just say that neither Malcolm nor I were smart enough to remain completely still. We did that awful dance until I really needed him.

It was mid-March and with graduation in May, the getting-a-job frenzy was in full effect. I had my hopes set on a permanent, full-time gig at Neon Advertising, one of the most prestigious advertising firms in New York City. I'd been talking with a major player at the firm for over a year, and I'd had a preliminary interview in February. At the beginning of March, I had my second interview. If things went my way, I'd have a final interview in April.

That Friday afternoon, I got a call from Ronald Sterling, the hiring manager at Neon. I hadn't made the cut. I wasn't smart enough. Or maybe I wasn't creative enough. Maybe I just hadn't said enough. I didn't know what it was.

Warm tears trickled down my face. I hadn't expected them. I'd expected to work in the creative services department at Neon and run in a cool, chic crowd of creative beings in the Big Apple. I'd quickly fall in love with New York, just as I had with Doberville. I'd live a life full of glamour and artistic epiphanies. Now that was all gone. I'd put all of my eggs in one basket that some other, brighter student had stolen.

I called my parents who did the whole, "I'm not going to tell you I told you so, but I told you to expand your options" – a paradoxical sentence to say the very least. That short-lived conversation left me more than sad. I was mad.

So I turned to what I hoped would be open arms. I called Malcolm, still in tears. As usual, he must have been too busy to pick up. He returned my call an hour later.

"I got your voicemail. I'm really sorry to hear the bad news," he empathized.

"I just don't understand. I thought it was a sure thing. Or at least an almost sure thing."

"You just have to pick yourself up and look for something better."

"Something better like what?"

"I don't know, Kelly. You'll find something."

"I've wanted this job since I started advertising."

"You'll find something. I promise. But, Kelly, can I call you back? I'm sort of in the middle of a project."

"Bye," I yelled, flustered. "And don't you dare call me back," I said to myself after hanging up. Malcolm only had time for himself.

Tired from tears unwisely spent, I settled on my bed for a late afternoon nap. It was almost ten o'clock when I awoke. As I pried my eyes open, I remembered that I'd lost the opportunity of a lifetime, or at least what felt like it. A new wave of sadness washed over me. My phone buzzed, and I lazily stretched across the bed to reach it.

"What's up?" read a new text message from Tayo.

"I didn't get the job," I responded. Tayo knew about my dream job. In fact, he knew all of my dreams.

"Damn... what are you doing?"

"I'm wallowing, as I should be."

"Who says? I'll be in the city in a few minutes. A friend and I are going out. Join us."

"I don't know that I'm really up to it." He didn't reply. I put on a slow rhythm and blues playlist and turned my attention to the ceiling. Then I tried counting sheep. When that didn't work, I heard a knock on my door.

"Not here," I yelled.

"Yes you are. Open up," Tayo said. I had no idea how he got into The Villas that night. Visitors had to be checked in and escorted by a resident. But there he was like a knight in shining armor. And I was his damsel in distress. I peered at him through the peephole.

"I thought you said you were with a friend," I said through the door.

"He's in the car."

"Well, I don't really feel like going out tonight."

"Just open the door, please." After wiping my eyes and brushing my hair into a ponytail, I opened the door. Tayo held out his arms and for a quick second I slipped into them. Then he drew away and held me at arm's length. "You need shoes and a jacket."

Without any further discussion, I put on my red Converses and off white bubble vest. "Where are we going?"

"Downtown. You need a drink." He looked me over once more. "Or two." I hiccuped. It was the start of a laugh. I hadn't laughed in hours, maybe not all day.

When we got to the car, I met Tayo's friend, Jeremy. He was comfortably stretched out and apparently asleep in the backseat.

"Wake up." Tayo poked him. "This is Kelly."

"Hey, Kelly. I saved you the front seat. Tayo wanted me to sit up there with him. But I said 'no, no, I'll let the little lady sit in the front.'"

"Well, let me know if you change your mind." I finally laughed.

Tayo and Jeremy worked hand in hand to keep that laughter afloat. Jeremy was your typical class clown, and Tayo did everything but tickle my toes to induce laughter. Calculating in the drinks Tayo bought me, I was gradually feeling less upset and more warm and fuzzy.

I sat at the bar and watched Tayo do the most ridiculous dances. Realizing that he'd do much better with a partner, he called me over.

"But you're doing so well all by yourself," I argued. He silently shook his head and crossed his arms in a serious effort to pout. It reminded me of the face my brother used to make when I hid his Hot Wheels toys.

I stood up and walked to him but refused to dance. He didn't need me to. He did all of the moving with one arm around my waist and the other free to assist him with his moves.

"You're offbeat!" I chuckled.

"Well, help me get on!" I began to move with him. And as usual, we were in sync, on beat, and right on time. We'd found our rhythm... again. That made me realize what I was missing with Malcolm – that carelessly easy connection. It made me realize just how much I had with Tayo. Sure we were physically attracted to each other, but above everything else, we were friends.

That night Tayo provided me a shoulder, then did everything he could so I didn't feel the need to cry on it. Maybe we didn't think alike. I was a bit of a black nationalist, and he preferred light-skinned women. But there was something keeping us in touch. My guess is that we walked to the beat of the same drum.

Whoever "the one" was, he had to share my rhythm and walk in stride with me. By the end of the night, Malcolm was out like a cigarette in the rain, and Tayo and I were on again.

But as in step as we were, I couldn't say that Tayo was the one. Sometimes I wanted him to be. But if he wasn't, I hoped we'd stay in touch. We'd be the embodiment of that Gwen Stefani song "Cool."

CHAPTER TEN: MY BLACK BROTHER

Love comes in different shapes and sizes – and colors, of course.

The weather was beginning to warm. I sat outside a small coffee shop near campus that blended in with the rowhouses surrounding it. Its white brick walls were peeling, and the wooden steps that led to the door creaked, but the coffee was rich and the price was right. The sun peeked in through perfectly blue clouds as I thought about Malcolm. I didn't miss him. Not one bit. I found that strange.

As I sipped my dark coffee, a black man approached me. His jeans were torn and his hair unkempt. When he smiled, I noticed his teeth were yellow and crooked. I picked up the book I'd been ignoring, and cast my eyes down to the crisp white pages.

"Sweetie," he said, "can I have a sip?"

"Sorry," I replied, without lifting my eyes.

"Can I taste it? Can I smell it?" he asked. "I'd give it to you. You'd never stop coming. It's that big. I'd marry you, you know." I felt the rage inside me swell, but I kept my nose in the book. I considered packing my bag and walking away. But who would I be to let this fool drive me away from my perfect seat in the sun? Not my mother's child. I stayed put.

"All I wanted was a taste. You think you're too good, don't you? Are you scared of me? Are you scared of the black man? Humph."

As he walked away, I slowly lifted my eyes from the unread

pages.

They called us angry, black women. They didn't understand why we had insurmountable walls and high voltage fences. Well, wouldn't you be angry if you couldn't sip your coffee without being harassed? If you couldn't ride the bus in peace because some man keeps sticking out his tongue at you in the most suggestive way? Well, wasn't he my black brother? And didn't I have the right to be mad?

That man had treated me no differently than he would a two-dollar whore. But even worse, he'd accused me of being scared of the men I've shown nothing but love. Maybe what made us angriest was being accused of not loving them, not loving them enough, not expressing our love, or not loving them properly. We just so happened to be as intricate and dynamic as they were, but they chose to cast that off as us being difficult.

They weren't all like that. The brothers, I mean. My biological brother wasn't like that. He was kind, friendlier than most, and extremely thoughtful – just like my father. To him, the world was a puzzle that he was slowly putting together. He was fairly quiet but never shy, and he was as smart as a whip.

I missed my brother, Kelvin. I was excited because in two days he'd be here to visit. It would be his first time in Doberville, and I had it all planned out.

He'd go to class with me on Friday to hear my favorite professor lecture. Then, we'd party all weekend long. Davis' annual White Party formally introduced spring, and I'd bought the perfect all-white outfit for the occasion weeks ago. The party was this Saturday, which was also April Fools' Day, but I wasn't worried about any pranksters because I'd have the perfect date, my brother.

Davis in the spring was why students survived the winter. Every student knew they just had to get through the biting cold and dreary days for a few months, then they could come out of hibernation to the sight of coeds lounging on blankets in the courtyard, music blaring in the middle of day, and everyone basking in the newfound sunlight. It was the time of year that professors fretted as they knew attendance would start to drop for no other reason than the weather. It was just too nice outside to sit in class all day long. We were all guilty of it.

I knew my brother would regret his decision to attend Georgia Tech after visiting Davis in the spring. After all, Davis in the spring was a season unto itself.

Kelvin's flight was due to arrive at ten in the morning on Friday. DJ had agreed to drive me to the airport to pick him up. I spoke to Kelvin that Thursday night to make sure that he was packed and ready to go.

"I think I'm more excited than you are. Why am I more excited than you?" I asked.

"I'm excited Helter Kelter. I promise." My brother was Mr. Cool. Like my father, he never showed an abundance of emotion unless the Falcons were playing.

"And you have a white button-down packed for the White Party, right?"

"It was the first thing I packed."

"Ok. I'll see you tomorrow. Do NOT miss your flight!"

I was practically bouncing up and down when DJ pulled his car around to the front of The Villas the next morning. "Right on time. Thanks, Deej."

"What's your brother's name again?" he asked.

"Kelvin. All Ks. Karol. Kelly. Kelvin. My parents are cornballs."

"Does he drink?"

"I don't think so. He may have had a drink or two in life, but I know he's never been sloppy drunk." DJ laughed.

"You have to leave him with us for a night."

"You and Matthew?" I laughed with him. "No way. No way I'd let you corrupt my brother."

"It's around this time boys become men."

"Just drive, DJ," I said, rolling my eyes.

When we arrived at the airport, I immediately spotted the thin, dark skinned boy I relentlessly teased as a child. I jumped out of the car and ran to him, but instead of throwing my arms around him, I stepped back and put my hands on my hips. He really had become a man at some point. He had facial hair. He was too cute. I didn't like the fact that he was THAT cute.

"Looking a little scruffy, aren't you?"

"I missed you, too," he said with a laugh. I finally gave him a hug. Then I reached for his luggage. When he objected, I insisted.

"I've got it. Besides, we have to hurry. DJ's waiting. You know how sluggish you are. I don't need you carrying anything other than your own weight."

"Always the drama queen," he said, swiping his bag from me and picking up the pace.

When we got to the car, I introduced him to DJ. DJ didn't

hesitate to ask him a million and two questions.

"How old are you, Kelvin?"

"18."

"Senior in high school?"

"Yep. Graduating and going to Georgia Tech in the fall."

"Aha. You chose to follow Karol instead of Kelly."

"Nah. I'm not following Karol either. I just happen to be going to her alma mater. Anyway, Helter Kelter's my favorite sister." When Kelvin was around me, I was always his favorite. He told me to keep it our little secret. And it was.

"Ok. What are you going to be studying?"

"Computer science."

"Ok. Sounds good. Do you drink?"

"Not regularly, but I'm willing to do anything to help Kelter have fun this weekend."

"I bet," I said. "The boys are going to take it easy on you, right, Deej?"

"Yeah, yeah. Got a girlfriend, Kelvin?"

"Yeah, a new one."

"What?" I asked, whipping my head around the seat. "What happened to Stacy?" Stacy was literally the girl next door. She'd been Kelvin's best friend since grade school. Even then she was as cute as a button.

Stacy was caramel complexioned with shoulder-length hair that she kept perfectly styled. From what I remember, she was the star of her class. She was the girl who all of the guys wanted to date. But Kelvin, smart yet unassuming, was always her number one.

"What do you mean? We're just friends."

"Kelvin, that girl likes you. She's always liked you. You're just... slow."

"Give your brother some credit, Kelly. He was quick enough to snag a different girl," DJ laughed.

"I need to see a picture when we get back to the dorm," I said, ignoring DJ. "There's no way she's as cute as Stacy."

There was no time to talk about his new girlfriend when my brother and I got back to the dorm. We were in a rush to make it to my favorite professor's lecture on time. Afterwards, we met Tamika and Brianna for lunch.

"I bet they don't have soul food at Georgia Tech," I said. Davis served fried catfish, collard greens and macaroni and cheese every Friday. I knew macaroni and cheese was Kelvin's favorite.

"That's why you have to visit me. Bring some of mom's best with you."

"Yep. Because we all know that Kelly does not cook," exclaimed Tamika with a laugh.

"Uh huh. That's why you don't have a man," added Brianna.

"I wouldn't mind cooking for him. I just have to find him first," I pleaded my case.

"What happened to Tayo?" asked Kelvin. He was one of the few guys I'd mentioned by name to my brother.

"We're just friends, Kelvin. You know that."

"Oh. Sorta like me and Stacy?"

"My brother has a new girlfriend," I clued in Tamika and Brianna. "He just gave up his love-and-basketball-esque sweetheart. Who does that?"

"Well, your brother's too cute to be on the market," Brianna said with a wink. "Too bad if this Stacy wasn't smart enough to scoop him up."

"What's her name? Your girlfriend, I mean," asked Tamika.

"Rosa."

"That's a pretty name," beamed Tamika.

"Weren't you supposed to show me a picture?" I prodded Kelvin. "Let's see her." He took out his phone and searched for her picture.

"I actually think you'd like her, Helter Kelter. She's a lot like you. Stubborn. Headstrong." He handed me the phone.

"Kelvin..." I said slowly, in disbelief. "She's not... black. What is she?"

"Filipino."

"Filipino?" I asked with a start. "What? You couldn't find a black girl?"

"Your brother has the right to date anyone he chooses, Kelly. So she's Filipino," Tamika said, shrugging her shoulders.

"So, she should be black, right, Brianna?" I looked for confirmation.

"Yeah. Sorry, Kelvin. I'm on Kelly's side here. There aren't any attractive *black* girls at your school?"

"There are," Kelvin and I said in unison.

"There are," Kelvin went on. "I love black girls. Rosa just happens to be Filipino."

"Do Mom and Dad know?" I interrupted him.

"They love her. Probably because she's so much like you. If they didn't love her, it'd be safe to say that they don't love you."

Everyone laughed – everyone except me.

"You can't be mad at the boy for liking a girl who's just like you, Kelly," Brianna said.

"I thought you were on my side?" I questioned her. She shrugged her shoulders. "Maybe I will let you hang out with DJ and Matthew tonight," I joked. "Maybe their taste will rub off on you."

I liked to think I chose DJ and Matthew as friends because we stood on the same principles. They were both into black culture and black girls like I was into black culture and black guys.

"I could use a night out with the guys."

"Listen to him. 'I could use a night out with the guys,'" I mocked. "He doesn't know what he wants." My brother just needed to meet a nice, black college girl. This *Rosa* was toast.

That night I let Kelvin go to Lemon and Salt with DJ and Matthew, but only after making sure that Duane wouldn't be with them. I planned to meet up with them later with Tayo.

When Tayo and I arrived at the bar, I regretted my decision to leave my brother with DJ and Matthew. He was drunk. They all were.

Kelvin, half slumped in his stool, sat in between two girls. He was chattier than I'd ever seen him. DJ was on the dance floor, whispering sweet nothings into Chassidy's ear. Matthew was ordering more drinks at the bar, apparently for Kelvin and the two girls he sat in between. I tapped Matthew on the shoulder.

"What round is this?" I asked.

"Hey, Kelly! Want a drink?"

"I'll take Kelvin's. I think he's had enough."

"Tayo. Didn't even see you back there. What's up?"

"Nothing. I'm chillin'. What's up with you?" Drinks in hand, we made our way to the table where Kelvin and the girls sat waiting.

"Just trying to graduate," shrugged Matthew.

"Helter Kelter!" Kelvin exclaimed. "My favorite sister. Sasha, I want you to meet my sister."

"It's Sarah," said the girl to the right of Kelvin with a smirk.

"This is Tayo. Tayo, this is Kelvin," I said, ignoring Kelvin's awkward introduction. They did that hand gesture that all black men seem to do, the one where they clasp hands instead of shaking.

Everyone got along well, drinking and joking. Soon my

brother began to sober, and I began to buzz. DJ and Chassidy joined us at the table as we rehashed stories from freshman and sophomore year.

Matthew was the first guy I'd met at Davis and he'd kept his title as the sweetest. DJ was nerd gone cool. When and where DJ found his cool was still up for debate. I was the girl that took them months to figure out – Miss Mysterious.

After countless stories, it was three o'clock and time to head home. The rest of the group went to McDonald's for a late night snack, leaving my brother and me to walk home alone.

"Did you have fun tonight?" I asked him.

"Yeah. You've got some cool friends."

"I knew you'd like them. DJ's an only child. I think he wants to adopt a brother."

"I don't need any brothers. You're close enough." He nudged me, and I tripped. Still tipsy, he'd thrown my balance.

"Thanks, I think. You guys didn't do anything too crazy without me, did you?"

"No. We had some drinks at Matthew's place. Picked up those girls. I think they were Matthew's friends. And then we came here."

"I'm glad I met up with you guys. If I hadn't, you'd be three sheets to the wind."

"It's the college experience I'm bound to get sooner or later."

"Later," I said with authority.

"Yes, ma'am," he teased. "No drinks at the White Party tomorrow night?"

"They won't be serving drinks. It's a school function. But anyway, did DJ tell you –"

"Hold on," he cut me off. "That's my phone."

"At three in the morning?"

"Rosa," he mouthed after picking up the phone.

"Let me speak to her," I said, wiggling my fingers for the phone.

"Rose, my sister wants to speak to you… Yeah. One second." He handed me the phone.

"Good night," I said with a laugh and a click.

"Did you just hang up on her?"

"Yeah," I giggled.

"It's not funny, Kelly." It was the first time since he arrived that he called me Kelly instead of Helter Kelter. Instantly, I knew he was mad. I wanted to take it back. But instead, I pressed forward. As if *he* was in the wrong.

"Didn't you like any of the girls tonight?" I asked. "What? Are you planning on taking a girlfriend to college with you?" We stood at the door of my dorm room. He wasn't listening to me. He was sending someone a text message. Probably Rosa.

"Being black and proud, which by the way, I am too, doesn't give you the right to be a rude little brat. I'm tired, and I'm going to sleep." He opened the door and went inside. I, speechless, let the door shut in my face. I just stood there in silence.

When I went inside, I found Kelvin curled up in his sleeping bag. I changed into pajamas and folded down my covers. I knew I wouldn't sleep well, knowing he was mad at me.

"Kelvin," I tried to wake him. "I'm sorry," I said, thinking maybe he hadn't fallen asleep yet. When he didn't reply, I lay down and eventually forced myself to go to sleep too.

When I woke up the next morning, Kelvin's sleeping bag was neatly rolled at the foot of my bed. He was nowhere to be found. I tried calling his cell and became anxious when I noticed it vibrating on my desk.

Ten minutes and a shower later, I heard a tap on my door. It was Kelvin, out of breath and dripping sweat. I'd forgotten that he ran every morning. I guess I thought he'd be hung over and lethargic like me. I decided I'd jump right into things.

"Kelvin, about last night –"

"I get it. I thought about it on my run this morning. And I'm not mad at you, Helter Kelter. A lot of guys do like women just because they're exotic-looking – women with light skin and long, wavy hair. But, I think black women are beautiful. And if the choice was mine, I would have chosen to fall in love with a black woman just because I know that's what you want for me. But I don't think I chose Rosa. It just happened."

"You really think you're in love?" I squealed. "My kid brother's in love?"

"Well, whatever it is," he shrugged.

I leapt to give him a hug and barely stopped short of his sweaty body.

"Go get in the shower. We have things to do today."

"Alright, Helter Kelter. Don't be such a drama queen," he said, flicking sweat off his forehead and in my general direction.

I wished his relationship with Rosa well. But if things didn't work out, I couldn't deny hoping his next love would be a black woman. People might grimace at the thought of such a wish, but when it seemed like every guy of your own didn't love his own, well, what would you have to say about that?

I made sure that Kelvin knew that I had his back, either way. He didn't choose my boyfriends, or else I'd probably be with Tayo. And I couldn't choose his girlfriends. That was the deal.

The White Party started at seven that night. But like everyone else, Kelvin and I were aiming to be fashionably late. At eight o'clock we were almost ready. I had on my new white linen pants with an ivory satin top. Kelvin wore dark denim jeans with the white button-down I'd advised him to pack. He was the perfect arm candy.

"You look great, Kelvin. Almost ready?"

"I'm waiting on you."

"Great. Let's head out. Tamika and Brianna said they would meet us downstairs."

The White Party was always held in the so-called Canyon, located down a flight of steep steps from the courtyard and enclosed by the Greek houses.

That night, the Canyon was decorated with small white tents surrounding a large wooden dance floor. DJ was spinning on the ones and twos. Food trucks lined the outer edge of the party.

In an hour, everyone would be on the dance floor. But in the meantime, students were either eating or chatting. The ones chatting were most likely praising each others' outfits. I had to admit the attire didn't fall short that year. Girls wore everything from long white maxi dresses to fringed white daisy dukes. Not an accessory missed or a curl out of place. The guys dressed just as well. Many had put on crisp white button-downs after seeing the barber that morning. The ones without fresh fades had neatly pulled up their locks.

The food ran out quickly. That never failed. The people who came to eat, came early. Knowing that we hadn't made the cut, we joined the minglers. Fifteen minutes in, George had stolen Tamika and I had lost Brianna. So I was happy to have my brother. I introduced Kelvin to tons of guys, who didn't pass him a second glance, and tons of girls, who asked who he was before I had a chance to tell them.

An hour later and right on time, students made their way to the dance floor. We did every dance that was hip at the time, and then there were the line dances – Davis culture at its finest. The electric slide was just the beginning. Davis students also knew the cupid shuffle, the New Orleans bunny hop, Detroit's ballroom and the cha cha slide. I was taking the time to teach it all to Kelvin. He caught on quickly, which came as no surprise to me.

There was something about a Davis party that brought everyone together. Midway through, I found myself dancing with Kevin despite his lack of kissing skills, and I'd even spoken to Duane. When it came to me, he'd become a man of few words. So his, "Nice outfit, Kelly," was sort of a big deal. Even Greg, who hardly ever took his face out of a book, was there. He didn't dance but he knew all of the words to the oldies DJ played. He also got along great with Kelvin.

We knew the party was over when DJ played Maze's "Before I Let You Go." It was always the last song played, and you weren't really a Davis student unless you knew all of the words. It was a feel good but bittersweet song as it meant the party was over. Many sang the lyrics to their boyfriends or their best friends. But the seniors sang to the good times we had at Davis, our last White Party and our last Davis in the spring.

I was sad to see Kelvin leave the next morning. We'd all miss him. He fit in perfectly with all of my friends. I thought about his relationship with Rosa. How he was doing what I couldn't. Or at least what I wouldn't. He was dating outside of his race, and he seemed happy.

It became my understanding that love either turned you sweet or bitter. If you were in love and everything was on the up and up, love had no choice but to trickle off of you so you became the definition of sweet. But if that love took a turn for the worst, you began to withhold it from everyone. Before you knew it, you were as bitter as a strong brew of beer.

Black men seemed to be receiving their love, and from every nationality out there. But, were we, black women, receiving ours? I believed men loved us. They really did. They loved the fullness of our features from our lips to our thighs. They loved the strength of our brawn and brains. But just as it was in the Antebellum South, some of them only loved us in private. Some of them just didn't want to take us public. We were their best-kept secret, their guilty pleasure. And let me tell you, that wreaked havoc on a girl. So, were we that strong brew of beer? Probably.

I couldn't help to think that maybe my brother got it right – not by dating outside of his race but by not limiting himself to his race. I didn't know that I'd ever been in love. And I couldn't say that Kelvin had either or that I liked that his girlfriend wasn't black. But anyone could see that my brother was as sweet as ever, and I was a little bit bitter. I'd have to find a man who could handle a strong brew. Who wanted a lightweight anyway? I shrugged my shoulders. What a weekend. At the end of it, I thought about how much I loved Kelvin. Hell, I loved all of my black brothers.

CHAPTER ELEVEN: MR. WORLD WIDE WEB

I could honestly say that I loved brownies. They're small, they're sweet, and they don't pack a punch.

I hated guys like Julian. That feeling you got when you first met an impressive, single guy... that feeling was unshakeable. It all went back to "new booty syndrome." That was why girls got attached so easily, wasn't it? We just couldn't shake that initial attraction. "But he was so cute, so nice, so funny the other day," was what we kept telling ourselves. So when said impressive guy had a drastic flaw and the red flag was thrown, we felt a quick punch to the gut. It almost proved just as bad as a difficult breakup when it happened over and over again. At the end of it all, we were black and blue from the bruises.

I'd recently started doing things alone. Eating out alone. Shopping alone. Working out alone. I realized I didn't always need or like company. But how ironic was it that being alone granted me a lot of attention? I heard that guys found it much easier to approach females when they flew solo, and such hearsay had since been confirmed.

As I nibbled on a banana nut muffin at a small café a couple of blocks from campus, I heard a voice behind me.

"19 nuts."

I turned around to see a guy not much taller than me. 5'6" maybe.

"I'm sorry?" I said.

"There are 19 nuts. Approximately 19 in each muffin. I count the nuts as I eat them. I love banana nut muffins." He took the seat across from me.

"You work here?" I deduced from his white apron and the pen and pad he kept half tucked in his pocket.

"I do. Where do you work?"

"Are you on break? Or are you always this... comfortable at work?" I ignored his question.

"Both," he answered. "Are you always this blunt?"

"When people I don't know sit at my table, yes." I shifted my weight away from him.

"Should I leave?"

"What's your name?" I ignored that question too.

"Julian Bateri. And you're Kelly"

"Have we met?" I asked in confusion.

"No. I overheard you impersonating your mom on the phone. What does she say again? 'Kelly, give your brother a break.'" He laughed. "Who were you talking to?" It was funny how much people could gather about your life when you were on the phone in public.

"My sister. My brother has a new girlfriend, and I've been going back and forth about how I feel about her. My mother thinks I'm being ridiculous, and maybe she's right. But my sister, Karol, is definitely on my side."

"Aha."

"Do you have any siblings?"

"One older brother. But we're not too close. We have different fathers. Have you tried our apple pie?" He noticed that I'd finished my banana nut muffin.

"I haven't. Is it any good?"

"I wouldn't have asked if it wasn't. It's the best thing on the menu, next to the muffins of course. One slice of apple pie and a cup of fresh squeezed lemonade?" he looked to me for confirmation. I nodded. "Coming right up."

He was right about the pie. Somebody had really put their foot in it.

"How is it?" he asked after clearing a few tables.

"Mmmm" with a smile was all I managed because of my full mouth.

"Drink," he laughed while pointing toward my full cup of lemonade. I took his advice and was pleased that the lemonade was just as impressive. Sweeter than sour. Just like I liked it.

"You must have read my mind." I pointed to my empty plate. "I needed that."

"Julian!" his manager called. "Stop flirting with that girl for a second." I blushed. "Dan needs help in the kitchen."

"Yeah, I should get going anyway," I said, "before you fatten me up and I get too comfortable."

"Can I call you sometime?" he asked.

"That would be ok." Just like that I'd met another guy. As I walked home I wondered whether or not he'd be different from the rest.

When I got home, I couldn't help but Google "Julian Bateri." I convinced myself that it wasn't stalking. It was simply cutting to the chase. If he had a girlfriend, I would like to know sooner rather than later. If we didn't have any of the same interests – books, movies, music, etc – I was saving myself the time of finding that out three or four dates in. Not to mention, you could find out a lot about a man through his Facebook status and Twitter updates. And don't even get me started on the uploaded photos. That saying, "A picture is worth a thousand words," had never been so true. Those photos that guys took of themselves in the bathroom with their shirts off – deal breakers.

But the online version of Julian Bateri didn't seem so bad. I found an article about him from his high school days. He'd played varsity baseball in a small city in Maryland. He'd been good enough to receive a full scholarship to Maryland College. Not too shabby. Actually, the article upped his cool points. I liked an athletic man, especially an athletic man in those tight pants that baseball players wore.

I'd Googled a guy before and received worse results. Much worse. His police report popped up. Call me overly cautious and a little judgmental, but I didn't return his phone calls. Another time, I Googled a guy and almost spilled the beans on our first date.

"So how do you like Doberville so far? You just moved here from Texas, right?" I remembered asking. No doubt something I'd read on his Facebook page, but I hadn't befriended him because I didn't want to look too eager.

"Did I mention that I just moved from Texas?" His face contorted.

"You did. Didn't you?" Awkward pause. "Or maybe Sam did." Sam was the mutual friend that had introduced the two of us. "Yeah, it was definitely Sam now that I think about it." His face relaxed just as I exhaled. Thank God I had Sam to get me out of that one.

I had even Googled myself to see what would pop up if a guy did. Guys could be nosy too, and you never knew if they used the same resources as women. I was ok with what a guy would find – some advertising photos, my Facebook page which was private so he'd only see my picture and the bare minimum of information about me, and a few of my records from running the hurdles in high school. But that was only if you included my middle initial and hometown or Davis University in your search.

Julian had listened in on my phone call, so Googling him made us even. Honestly, what did people do before the Internet? Some said it was risky to meet someone on the Internet, but I would say it was just as risky to go out with someone without Googling him first.

I had an economics quiz the next morning. I was encouraged because I'd done much better on my last one with a B-plus – just short of an A. But to be honest, grades didn't mean as much to me anymore. With graduation in sight, I was no longer at risk of losing my scholarship, and a couple of Bs wouldn't drop my grade point average that much. Guys were what I needed to focus on.

I knew once I graduated from college, my options would only go farther downhill for male companionship. Let's face it. We had all heard the stories about how few men you met after graduation. Here was the scenario. You landed a well paying job at a highly esteemed company where there was opportunity for career growth. But after attending the company holiday party or joining the company softball team, you realized that you were one of the few African Americans that worked there. While your coworkers got engaged, you found yourself attending weddings without the plus one. So, you either (a) went back for leftovers, back to old boyfriends or flames that were only half lit; (b) downgraded, ending up with the nice guy who never got his degree, never found a skill or a personality, neither cooked nor cleaned, and had no desire to leave his eight dollar an hour job; or (c) stayed single and hoped to one day meet the man of your dreams, which was a long shot that would likely leave you eighty and living with a dozen cats.

With those scenarios in mind, I received a text message from Julian.

"Nice to meet you. Let's Skype sometime soon- Julian_Bateri."

I gave him my Skype name and from that point on we were in business.

The next day was a Tuesday. As usual, I found myself sleepily pitching reporters while sipping on a Diet Coke at my internship. Everything I ate back in college was unhealthy. So I went for the Diet Coke in a fifty percent effort to make my drink intake nutritional. On one hand, I could've gone for a bottle of water or an apple juice, but on the other I could've gone for a regular Coke. I convinced myself that the diet drink put me somewhere in the middle. Same with the 100-calorie pack of cheese nips I munched on.

My stomach was growling when I got back to my dorm. The soda and cheese nips hadn't done much. I popped some frozen fries and a few fish sticks into the oven. While I waited for them to warm, I started Faust, a play I had to read for my humanities class and opened a fresh Word document on my computer to take notes. But ten minutes into reading, as I sat in front of my computer with an open book on my lap, Julian rang via Skype for the first time.

After three rings, I answered.

"Hey there," I said.

"Hey. Glad I caught up with you. What are you doing?"

"I'm cooking." I know that was a bit of an embellishment. But he didn't. And technically I was cooking. Just not from scratch. "And I'm reading." I held up the book so he could read the cover.

"Hmm. Any good?" he asked.

"What? My cooking or the book?" I joked.

"Either," he retorted.

"I'd say they're comparable. Faust is a play that's been read and performed for years all over the world. And my cooking is... edible. What do you have going on?"

"I'm changing the color of my iPhone."

"You're doing what?" I had never heard of anyone changing the color of his iPhone. Frankly, I didn't know it was possible.

"I'm a technology junkie. I have to have the newest and the latest, even if it's just a cosmetic change. The new white iPhone is out so I'm giving my black one the upgrade. I ordered the parts off of the Internet a couple of days ago. They just came in."

"Wow. How long is it going to take you?"

"There are a lot of little screws here, but it's not so bad. Thirty minutes tops."

"You just may be my polar opposite. I barely know how to

turn this computer on." He laughed. "You think I'm joking?" I shook my head.

"Well, now you have someone to call if you ever need help. Or if you need someone to help you eat that meal you're making. What's for dinner?"

"Fish and chips." That sounded much better than fish sticks and fries. Who was I to break his heart if he thought I was making it from scratch?

Julian was easy to talk to and even easier on the eyes. He smiled seventy five percent of the time. Even as he spoke, his smile shone through.

I've always thought that men needed facial hair, and the more the merrier. It gave them that ruggedly sexy male appeal. And it defined their gender. In a world where it was becoming harder and harder to tell who was what, facial hair helped. It was the equivalent of a woman with manicured nails. It was that extra touch of femininity that made the men ogle. But there were a few, a very few, men who didn't need facial hair. They all had a pronounced facial feature that gave them their exception, like a strong jaw line. That was the case with Julian.

We became regular Skype buddies, and I began to expect his call. But after a week and a half of the back and forth, I was itching for the first date. I'd thrown out plenty of hints that he was either missing or ignoring.

You couldn't take in someone's cologne or natural scent over the Internet. I was very affected by the way that a man smelled. One of my guy friends crashed in my bed sophomore year. When he left the next morning, he forgot to take his smell with him. My fluffy blue decorative pillow smelled just like him for the next week. I spent that week taking in his scent and wondering if I was in love with him based on smell alone. It wasn't one of those recognizable scents, and that's probably because it wasn't too masculine. In my mind, the perfect male scent wasn't overly masculine. If you were a man and you exuded masculinity, your cologne didn't have to scream it. Anyway, that smell made me crazy about him for a whole week. After the smell waned, I went back to seeing him as just another one of my silly guy friends.

You could see him over Skype, but you couldn't breathe him in. Technology was great, but there was something to be said about actual face-to-face interaction.

I decided to be forthright with Julian. I asked him out, and he accepted. On Saturday night at eight sharp, we were to meet at

Davey's Bar and Grill downtown.

I was a little late, but he was on time. I found him at the bar sipping what he would later tell me was a Jameson and ginger. I liked the sight of him. He wore khaki bottoms and a fitted checkered button-down. His jacket hung on the back of his chair and his grey beanie carelessly sat on the leg that he'd bent so that his foot rested a few inches from the floor at the bottom of the stool. His other leg, wide apart from the first, was stretched out.

I wasn't a big drinker, but I did like a man who knew how and what to drink. I wasn't interested in a man who got sloppy drunk or couldn't hold his liquor. And I thought it was a little weird to see a man drinking a glass of white wine, a cranberry and vodka or a tequila sunrise. There was such a thing as a man's drink and the aforementioned didn't fall into that category. However, a Jameson and ginger, did.

I was a little nervous as I approached him. I put my hand on his shoulder and liked how warm it was.

"Drinking alone?" I asked.

"Not anymore," he answered. He gave me a light hug and led us to the host. "Table for two." I've always liked a man who could take charge and Julian was doing just that. He wasn't nervous or twitchy about it either. He was calm, smooth, a little snake-like. I would have to watch out for this one. He even ordered for me. I wanted the crab cake sandwich, remoulade sauce on the side, with a side salad, vinaigrette dressing. He articulated that perfectly to our server.

We learned that we had a lot in common. He'd lived in Atlanta for the first ten years of his life. That would explain the southern hospitality. He liked to read, mostly biographies and autobiographies. That would explain his vocabulary. He volunteered at the Boys and Girls Club, which meant that he liked kids. So did I. After I found *the one*, I was aiming to have at least five.

Julian was one of those guys who said all the right things. Either every girl liked to hear the same thing, or he was a pretty good tailor. The date was going so well that I was afraid that we looked like clowns with the smiles that we each had plastered on our face. His was natural and mine was induced. Neither was fading.

But I was a little sad when Julian called for the check, and even sadder with how quickly our server arrived with it. I was going to ask Julian to go get a cup of coffee when he slid the check over to me. Wait, that's not how things usually go. Was Julian asking me to pay? There was that quick punch to the gut.

"Oh, you need help with the check?" I asked. I found that asking a guy if he needed help with the check messed with his ego. Guys didn't like to ask for help with anything. I was hoping that my question would make Julian man up.

"Fifty-fifty is what I always say." I guess my little ego tactic didn't work on all of them.

I was always able to handle my portion of the check, but that was beside the point. The first date was all about first impressions. Men, what type of impression were you giving a lady when you asked for her credit card on the first date? A man not picking up the check showed a lack of effort. And if you weren't trying, why would I?

I took a good look at our server. He'd introduced himself as Larry. He was an attractive man, possibly a Davis student, present or former. There was an eighty percent chance that he was straight, fifty percent that he was single.

I didn't have too many ratchet stories because I generally didn't like to make too much of a fuss. But I found myself going there with this one. Asking a girl to pay on the first date was downright disrespectful. And since you reaped what you sow...

"Larry, before you take the check, can I ask you a question?" He looked hesitant.

"Sure."

"Do you have a girlfriend?" He looked uncomfortable.

"No."

"A boyfriend?" I raised an eyebrow. He frowned.

"Hell no. Ladies only."

"Well, then, you probably go on a few first dates here and there?"

"Yeah." He shrugged. Then nodded.

"Do you pay on the first date?"

"Always," he said quickly. Then he grimaced after realizing where I'd gone with that question, and that he'd sucker punched my date on accident. Julian sat on the other side of the table silently fuming. I guess he'd lost his slick dialogue.

"That's what I thought. My number is on the back of the check." And with that, Julian got up and I never heard from him again. I guess he knew he couldn't smooth talk his way with me after that. And he probably didn't want to anyway.

Larry and I laughed about it after he left. He said he'd served couples on their first date before but that he'd never seen things go awry so quickly. And neither had I. Julian seemed so perfect. But I guess that was one of those things that you couldn't Google. Maybe Facebook should make that part of the profile. Name. Gender. Age. Interested in. How often you pick up the tab.

I walked home with my leftovers. I didn't waste when it was coming out of my own pocket. I also had the free dessert that Larry threw in for me. I guess the date wasn't so bad after all. I did love brownies.

I ran into Tamika a few blocks from The Villas.

"Hey, girl. How was your date?" she asked.

"A hot mess. Where are you headed?"

"CVS run. I think my suitemate is eating our toilet paper. That would be the only explanation."

"Well, I'm pretty sure that my suitemate doesn't even use toilet paper. Consider yourself lucky."

"I guess. Are you going to be in your room later? I sorta have something to tell you."

"Probably. I think I'm going to take a quick nap."

Instead of napping, I lay awake thinking about Julian. He was in and out of my life like a flash of lighting. Surprisingly, I wasn't that mad about it. For so long, I'd felt that anyone who didn't live up to my standards, didn't share my mindset, didn't want what I wanted was a waste of time. For the first time, I considered these flawed men a blessing.

If nothing else, they'd help me pass the time. Malcolm had taken me for my first falafel. Even Blake, the drastically flawed boyfriend I'd kept in high school, had taken me on my first date and taught me how to drive a stick. I named my first car after him. I still kept in touch with about half of my exes, though Julian wouldn't be in that half. That scored me a free frappuccino at Starbucks, a ticket to see the Nationals play the Braves, a free brownie to go or a funny dating story if nothing else. Former dates had expanded my network. Larry, my new favorite sever, was now in it.

CHAPTER TWELVE: THE DEAL SEALER

Love was quietly right beside me. Like most people in power, it didn't have to scream its presence.

Chemistry. Passion. Fireworks. Sparks. Those were the words that women used to describe the way they felt about their man. It was those words that I'd been looking for. They were the words I believed in. Anything short of them would never be love, so I thought.

"I just don't agree with you," my mother argued. Remember, she always sided with realism, not romance.

"What do you mean?"

"We use those words to tell a story. 'The chemistry was undeniable. Their passion for each other exhausting.'" She exhaled loudly. "Honey, please. Love is raw, and it comes in various sizes. Don't ask yourself if there's passion. Ask yourself, what's his soul like?"

I'd given Tamika a lot of shit about George. For weeks, now months, she'd used him as her stepping stool. So I thought she was on the rebound. But a couple of days ago she hit me with the "I think I'm in love" routine. That's what she had to tell me, and I laughed. What she had with George didn't seem to graze the feelings she had for DJ. Obviously, she wasn't happy with my reaction.

"You're telling me love exists without chemistry or passion?" I asked my mother.

"No. I'm asking you to rethink your definition of chemistry

and passion. They're different from obsession. Don't you think you have a choice in the matter? In who you love?"

"I don't know. I guess I haven't figured that out yet."

"We choose who we love. But choose wisely. And don't let things that are flighty sway your choice."

"You don't believe that Dad is your soul mate? That you were made for each other? You sound so unromantic."

And there was the question of soul mates again. I remembered a recent conversation I'd had with DJ.

"Is she your soul mate?" I'd asked him of Chassidy.

"I haven't given it enough thought."

"Do you believe in soul mates? Honestly?"

"Not anymore. It sounds nice." He paused. "Someone brought the idea of multiple soul mates to my attention. I haven't used the word since then because if you can have more than one, you can have many."

"Well, that's not very romantic," I laughed.

"You asked me to be honest, not romantic. I bet you believe in soul mates."

"I think so. You know me, Deej."

"Yes, I do." He shook his head.

I liked to believe that I had another half out there. That I'd meet him at Davis. That it would be our fate. Our destiny. But did it really work that way? It was one of those questions that I couldn't work through. Like which came first, the chicken or the egg? Did we create our destiny or was it manifest?

"Choosing to love someone forever is the most romantic thing you can do," Mom explained.

I wasn't convinced. I'd read too many romance novels to be convinced. But I *was* rethinking everything. Maybe I was wrong about Tamika and George. What did I know about love? I wouldn't know my soul mate if Cupid shot me in the heart with an arrow.

Because of my ignorance, there was tension between Tamika and me when it came to the George topic. But Brianna, Marcus and I had agreed to go to dinner with them, and it looked like there was no getting out of it. The plan was to meet outside of The Villas at six o'clock.

I was the first one there. I looked around and saw Tamika and George waving to me from the other side of the road. I noticed how in stride they were as they approached.

"Look who's on time. I guess I owe you five bucks, George,"

Tamika laughed.

"Oh, that's really funny." Tamika took a five out of her handbag and slid it into his pants pocket. "Cute Mika. Now, where are Marcus and Bri?" I asked.

"Marcus said he'll meet us there," George answered.

"And Brianna's coming from work. She said she'll meet us there too," Tamika added.

Great. I was left alone to make the walk with the love birds. At least it was a short walk to the restaurant. They were holding hands and I was just... there, uncomfortable to say the least. I had a very strong fear of being the unwelcomed third wheel, and they were bringing that fear to the surface. Tamika and George might as well have been whistling and skipping beside me. But a few blocks and eye rolls later, we were there.

Black people seemed to be addicted to soul. Soul mates. Soul music. Soul train. Soul food. We ended up going to Wonder-Soul Cafe, a little hole in the wall soul food place a few blocks from campus. If nothing else, the food would be good. They had the best chicken wings and macaroni and cheese in town.

We found Marcus there waiting, and I was unbelievably thankful to no longer be the odd man out. Marcus was the type of guy that could make the sun shine on a rainy day. He played that role in my life fairly often, starting with the bug that had put a damper on my day.

"Hey, babe. You look good. You're filling out nicely." Marcus told me this every time I saw him. I hadn't gained a pound.

"Another tattoo? What's this one?" I asked, checking out the inscription on his forearm.

"It's my grandmother's nickname. We were really close before she died a couple of years ago."

"That's very special," I said as he lifted me off the ground, hugging me close.

"You know I had to do it," he laughed. It wasn't unlike Marcus to pick me up and practically strangle me. I think he had a little crush on me. "Where have you been?"

"Just three doors down Marcus. You know where to find me." Marcus had found me a couple of times in the middle of the night. People would drop him off at my door as drunk as a skunk. It was as if he could never remember his own room number when he was drunk, so he gave out mine. I'd practically have to carry him down the hallway. Though Marcus was thin, he was 6'5". Helping him to his room wasn't easy, but I didn't mind because he was just as good of a friend to me. He liked to cook and he didn't mind sharing.

"You're right, sweetheart. Let's get something to eat, y'all. I'm starving."

"We're waiting on Brianna," Tamika said. Not a minute later, we heard Brianna before we saw her.

"I'm so over Kenny," she was yelling into the phone. "He's such an idiot. But I'm here so I gotta go, girl. I'll call you back later to tell you what this fool did." She made her way to us. "Hey, guys, let's eat."

We ordered our food and took it upstairs where there was room to sit down. Just as expected, the meal hit the spot. But the conversation had taken a turn for the worst.

"I don't know why you're not married, Kelly," Marcus said.

"Married? I'm only twenty two. I'm still in undergrad. No one is married."

"No, you know what I mean. No one's wifed you yet. You're definitely wifey material. I'd take you home to Mom's."

"Tell that to the guys that I've been dating."

"It's not just them, Kelly. It's you too," Tamika joined in.

"What?" I asked.

"You have unrealistic expectations. You think pigs are going to start flying for you." Who was this girl and what had she done with my best friend? Tamika had never called me out on my dating habits before. Why start now in front of a table full of people?

"I don't really know what gives you that idea," I responded.

"You gave Duane only four months before you pressured him to commit to you. He'd just ended a three year relationship." I guess I never mentioned that he and his ex had been together for three years.

"Well, it doesn't take four months to know if you like someone. I dodged a bullet with Duane anyway."

"What about Kevin?" she asked.

"What do you mean?"

"Kevin liked you and you dissed him after one kiss. And Darius, you plain ignored him for three months." She was hanging my underwear to dry... in public. "Look, I'm not saying that you date a bunch of prince charmings, but just give a guy a chance."

I figured it wasn't the best time to tell her my Julian story. I was beginning to see that this didn't have much to do with me though she may have had a point. She just wanted me to understand her relationship with George. So I backed down.

"Maybe you're right." She hadn't expected that. She didn't know what to say.

"If anyone is wifey material, it's me," Brianna said in jest. "Kelly, you can't cook. And Tamika, you're too messy. Have you cleaned your room this week? I don't know how you put up with it, George."

"You can put up with a lot when you love someone." Here they go again with this love talk. Marcus practically spit out his food. I guess it had been a while since he'd had a heart to heart with his boy.

"I need some water," he said, choking as he got up from the table. Marcus looked completely flushed when he came back, like he'd seen a ghost. I couldn't blame him. It wasn't easy losing your best friend to a significant other.

"So, what's going on with Kenny, Bri? We all heard you on the phone," I said.

"He sold his bed."

"What do you mean he sold his bed? For what?" We all laughed. "Where is he going to sleep?"

"He sold his bed for a pair of Jordans. You know, the new ones that just came out. And get this, he hasn't even worn them. Or at least I haven't seen them."

"Don't tell me that," exclaimed Marcus. He knew Kenny well. They weren't best friends, but they did run in the same circles occasionally. "For some Jordans? I don't even rock Jordans anymore."

"Well, Kenny thinks he's going to sleep in my bed for the rest of the semester. Said he was going to sell his bed after graduation anyway," Brianna said.

"Are you going to let him?" I asked.

"Not a chance," she answered insolently. "I can't stand it when he does stupid stuff like that, and I refuse to enable him."

"I think he was just looking for a reason to sleep with you every night. No pun intended," interjected Tamika.

"I'm not really sure I care about the reason," Brianna responded while sipping her Arnold Palmer. "Let's go get a real drink. Anyone up for it?"

We walked a couple of blocks down the street to a little dive bar where we ordered hard ciders and light beers. George and Tamika didn't stay long. They were there just long enough for the three of us to see how in love they were.

It wasn't anything exaggerated or overzealous. It was just the way he made sure she had somewhere to sit. There were only a few chairs at the bar so George, Marcus and I stood while Tamika and Brianna sat. George wasn't touching Tamika, but he stood close enough to her chair to mark his territory. It was the way he leaned across her to order their drinks. He hadn't even asked for her order. I guess he just knew.

Tamika was talking to Brianna about Kenny. George was talking to the guy in the chair next to Mika. It was the way they were talking to different people but still heard each other. Every now and then, one would jump in the other's conversation and then jump right back out. It was the way they both summed up those conversations and decided to leave at the same time.

Marcus, Brianna and I stayed. We had a good time mixing and mingling with the crowd. Marcus was always loud enough to draw people in. His laugh made people's heads turn. They turned and listened. After a minute or two, they found themselves laughing with him. Brianna was quite the crowd pleaser as well. She had a ton of jokes and as long as they weren't at your expense, you loved her instantly. Around those two, I'd be considered quiet. So there I sat, quietly sipping my third or fourth beer.

I was heavily tipsy, and Tayo was the only person I could think about. No matter how much I told myself that he just wasn't for me, he crept back into my mind and claimed it. Seeing George and Tamika together made me want what they had more than ever, and Tayo was the only one who I could imagine having it with.

He was the fan favorite, or at least he was the friend favorite. Everyone grounded was rooting for him. Team Tayo. I went back and forth between wanting him as a friend and wanting him for more. Maybe I'd be less undecided if I knew that he wanted to commit to me.

I felt like the stars were against me, and I was playing tug-of-war with fate. Fate was a hell of an opponent. Tamika was lucky to find George. They'd told us that night that he'd sealed the deal with a promise ring. They were an item, and that promise ring would probably turn into an engagement ring in a year or two.

Tayo wasn't the seal the deal type. At least he wasn't with me. Maybe it was timing. Or the sex thing. Or it was possible that he just didn't like me enough. I kept replaying what my mother had said about choosing to love someone forever. But you only have the power to choose for yourself. You can't make the one you love choose you back.

A couple of days shot by, and I found myself without much time to think about Tayo. It felt like the semester had just started but already finals were here. Sunday night was cram time, and the computer lab and each library on campus were packed to capacity. It would stay this way all night long. If it weren't for the lack of sunlight, you'd think it was midday.

Students in Davis sweats with unkempt hair gulped Red Bull and prayed to the high heavens to stay awake, mentally and physically. It was the one time of the year that girls put away their stilettos. People with contacts surprisingly wore their glasses. Guys traded in their Jordans and loafers for slide-ons. When you knew you wouldn't be getting a minute of shuteye, you dressed for comfort.

Tamika and I were among the bunch. She had a twenty-page paper due, and I had an economics final in twelve hours. The two of us were sort of back to normal. She'd been comfortable enough to borrow my North Face jacket without asking. That had to mean we were on the right track.

I sat in the library thoughtlessly staring at my economics book when I noticed Drew. I raised the book higher to shield my face. Drew had liked me since freshman or sophomore year and if he saw me sitting there I'd probably hear another plea to date me. I'd never said yes because there was something that I couldn't stand about Drew. I just couldn't put my finger on it.

I thought about what Tamika said about pigs flying for me. Should I have given a guy like Drew a chance? Were my standards really that high? I didn't think they were...

He had to know how to drive a stick, and there was nothing worse than a guy who couldn't parallel park. I'd like for him to be able to handle a strong masculine drink, and he should offer to pay for my girly white wine. He had to know how to give a proper handshake sans sweaty palms. Without the aforementioned traits, I clearly couldn't take him to the company holiday party. His ideal woman should be a black woman with black skin and black hair, basically, me.

Like my brother, he should know the definition of a man. Like my father, he had to know how to love because, honestly, some men just didn't know how. Unlike Kevin, he had to be a good kisser. Unlike Malcolm, he had to have time for me. Like Julian, he should be Google-friendly. Like Tayo, he should share my rhythm. Unlike Tayo, he should be able to express his feelings for me, which included being able to actually say he missed me. He needed to be as intelligent as my favorite professor. He had to know how to lead. When I found myself in a packed environment, the last thing I wanted was to be with a man who couldn't navigate. If he couldn't lead me through a crowd, why would I expect him to take the reins in any other way?

And then there was my scarf rule. I just didn't like to see a man in a scarf of any form or fashion. The same went for red pants and white-framed sunglasses, but the worst was light washed denim. Dark denim or khakis were the only way for men to be casual.

I didn't think it was cute to see a man dressed as a woman, ever... for any reason. It wasn't cute on Halloween. And I didn't make exceptions for actors. Sorry, Tyler Perry. My man stayed a man all day, every day.

If he expected me to cook, I expected the same of him. And if his mama was still washing his laundry, I took issue with that. But it was a plus if he still went to church with her every Sunday. He had to be a Christian. If he wasn't and we had kids, there was a divorce waiting to happen.

Since I was an artsy advertiser, my ideal man enjoyed math or science, complementing me. I imagined him as a mathematician, a scientist, an architect, an engineer, an economist, a pharmacist, some type of a doctor maybe. He was the type that could fix my computer or my car. But he appreciated the arts. He had to appreciate my work as well as the painting that hung above the couch in our living room.

The way he and I vibed in a social setting was a big deal to me. I thought a man should stick by me but not underneath me. He was confident enough to mix and mingle, but he never forgot whom he came with and whom he couldn't leave without. When he was with my family, he found a way to talk without putting his foot in his mouth. He was competitive enough to play card games with me for hours, but he was not a poor sport when he lost. He smiled in pictures. He enjoyed giving back rubs. And he put me on a pedestal.

Hmmm. The list was longer than I thought. I'd been so busy thinking about it that I hadn't noticed Greg sitting across from me. He looked comfortable, like he was in his natural habitat.

"What are you studying?" I asked him.

"Oh, I'm not studying. I'm just reading," he answered.

"Then what are you doing in the library?"

"Reading." He looked perplexed with the question. Maybe it did sound like a stupid question, but during cram time, there were no leisure readers. Everyone was in a panic to finish a paper or to learn a semester's worth of information in a night. Greg was the odd man out. He had no real work to do. The idea of him sitting there reading leisurely was equivalent to him sticking out his tongue at me.

"Go home," I said with a smile. But he didn't go. He just sat there across from me, and for over an hour we didn't speak until I saw him yawn.

"You're tired and you have nothing to do. What are you still doing here?"

"I'm keeping you company." Tamika looked up from her computer, something she hadn't done in hours. She laughed, shook her head and went right back to work.

"Well, ok. Just thought you might want to go to sleep. It's getting really late," I said.

"I don't sleep much anyway." So, he sat there across from me, reading. We didn't leave until around four in the morning.

I noticed Greg as I took my finals over the next couple of days. I found myself bumping into him a lot, and it dawned on me that it might not have been so coincidental.

I thought about the way Kenny had spontaneously sold his bed. And all of a sudden, I realized that these guys were panicking. At the end of the semester, they'd be leaving their best girls, boos, mains. I, of all people, knew what they were going through. I had only weeks left to find someone who would seal the deal. I guess you could say that some of us were in full panic mode.

CHAPTER THIRTEEN: THE PSYCHOLOGIST

***Even love has a starting point.
Could it start with a Skittle?***

He was really nice about saying that he didn't care about me.

"You're very smart and pretty, and I've cared deeply for a lot of smart and pretty women. But, you're just not one of them." I didn't know how to respond to that. How are you supposed to respond when someone you care for says that they don't care for you? I blinked.

I dated him for about six months last year, and those were his parting lines. In those last few weeks at Davis, I would finally experience what it was like to have a man, who wasn't obligated by blood, care for me. That feeling got into your psyche, and you couldn't settle for anything less.

For instance, there was a difference between a guy who couldn't keep his hands off of you and a guy who couldn't keep his hands off of your face, your hands, your hair. He studied all of your features. Memorized your moles. Calculated the length of your limbs.

Greg came over because he needed me to fill out a survey for him. It was for some last minute psych project, so he said. Psychology was the perfect major for Greg. He had a lot going on in that mind of his, much more than I'd like to know.

For a long time, I couldn't read Greg. He was just a recluse who liked to play his guitar. And for some reason, he didn't mind talking to me. That was pretty much all I knew.

Lamar introduced me to Greg. Lamar and I were close freshman year because he was dating a friend from home so we knew each other prior to Davis. He and I partied together. He shared his room when I got locked out of my own. We split Subway sandwiches. We laughed together. And Greg was somehow around for all of that.

I think Lamar overshadowed Greg a bit. He had much more conversation to offer, and he was one of Davis's best soccer players. His voice was deep, so deep that it almost echoed. So again, he had more of a presence. Greg was the type who snuck up on you. One day, you just knew him. One day, you were just comfortable around him. You didn't see it happening. You didn't know how it had happened. Although Lamar and I grew apart as the years went on, Greg stuck. Our friendship had grown. And so there Greg and I were in the last semester of our tenure at Davis.

I filled out his survey though I couldn't tell you what the questions were. What I could tell you was that it was an awkward night. I'd expected him to leave after I'd answered all of his questions. But he didn't. He put the form I'd filled out in his notebook and he just sat there. I took it upon myself to get a conversation going.

"So what are your plans after graduation?"

"I'm trying to get into grad school. Davis again. This time for education. What about you?"

"I have nothing planned. I'm a little strung out about it. I'm not too sure why I brought it up," I laughed. He laughed. And then we were quiet again.

"I like your nose," he said, interrupting the silence.

I didn't know what to say to that. Funny that I never knew what to say when I was being complimented or insulted, or even really what to think about it. I had always thought of my nose as just a means to breathe.

"It fits your face," he expounded. It was one of the strangest compliments I'd ever received.

"Thanks, Greg. Yours isn't so bad either." We sat face to face on my bed at that moment. I turned away because I was uncomfortable with his staring at my nose. Also, I was craving the half eaten bag of Skittles barely within arm's reach on my desk behind me. I was reluctant to turn back around to face him, but I did as I began to eat the Skittles.

"Can I have one?" he asked. Now, I considered myself a fairly nice person, and most of the time I didn't mind sharing. But there were four things that I did not share: my men, my closet, my Chipotle and my Skittles. It was an odd list, I know. But I'd politely learned how to explain this to people.

"If I had a second bag, it would be all yours. But I'm really a Skittle feign. It wouldn't be nice of you to take a Skittle, and it wouldn't be nice of me to resent you for it. So no, you can't have one. I'm sorry."

He put out his hand as if he hadn't heard anything I'd just said.

"I'm serious, Greg."

"You're really not going to give me one Skittle?"

"No, they're my favorite." I poured part of the bag into my hand and Greg reached for them. I closed my left hand around the loose Skittles and tightened my grip on the bag in my right.

"Are you really losing out by giving me one Skittle?" he asked.

"Are you really gaining?" I asked as he reached again, farther this time. I poured the loose Skittles into my mouth. "Too late," I said through a mouth full of Skittles.

"You still have the bag." He lunged for my arm and pulled it towards him. He tried to pry the bag from my hand, but he didn't stand a chance against my kung fu grip.

"I give up." He held his arms up in surrender. I relaxed my grip and just as quickly he'd stolen the bag.

"Give it back."

"Nope."

"You're so annoying."

"It's a bag of Skittles, not a bag of gold. Calm down." He handed me the bag back.

"I wasn't even mad." I smirked.

Then, he began to tickle me. I laughed when being tickled, but I got angry on the inside. I hated the feeling of squeezing my stomach so tight that it hurt. I did anything to make it stop. Kick. Scream. Bite. This time, I just let the bag go. And thank God, he stopped tickling me. But I found myself in a compromising position.

Then, he kissed me. They were the biggest lips that I'd ever touched mine to. I was a little surprised that they didn't swallow me whole and that I'd lived to tell the tale. And even more surprised that I liked telling it. I couldn't deny liking the way his lips met mine.

    Tamika was enthused and Brianna was confused.
    "You kissed Greg? Quiet and awkward Greg? The one from Tennessee?" Brianna asked.
    "Yeah," I answered.
    "And you liked it?" Brianna continued.
    "Yeah."
    "So what? You're going to start dating him now?" Tamika asked
    "Well, I'm going to start kissing him."
    "Then you don't really like him?" Tamika said disheartened.
    "I might." She lit up again.
    "So when's the next... moment?" she asked careful to not call it a date.
    "Maybe tonight. He's coming over."
    "For what?" Brianna asked.
    "I don't know. He asked if he could come, and I said yes. I didn't really question him."

    When I saw Greg that night, I found out why he'd asked to come over. He'd bought me a book.
    "What is this?" I asked.
    "It's a gift," he answered nonchalantly.
    "Well, thank you. But what's it for?"
    "You can call it a graduation gift."
    It was one of those "For Dummies" books on writing a novel.
    It was funny how someone that liked you found it easy to get to know you. In addition to memorizing the landscape of your body, he was involved in your thoughts.
    I remembered a conversation I'd had with Duane after running into two men singing in the tunnels of the transit system. I caught the two men in the middle of their rendition of "Loved by You" by Curtis Mayfield and the Impressions. I glanced down at the overflowing bucket of cash in front of them in awe. These two men, at least forty in age, were happily making their living singing for tired, overworked, tax-paying public transportation riders who rarely ever stopped during rush hour for anyone or anything. But we all stopped for them. They were dinner on the table after a long workday or an ice cream bar on a sweltering, summer evening. They were filling and refreshing. They were sharing a gift with me, and I had no gift in return to offer them.

"They were bomb, Duane. They reminded me of DJ."

"How so?"

"I don't know. There's just something about DJ when he plays his music. He becomes untouchable."

"You're like that when you talk about advertising. You're always dissecting some TV or radio advertisement. I like that about you."

"I don't know. Advertising is a career path for me. I'm not so sure I'd call it my passion."

He didn't say anything because he didn't get it. Duane and I had those moments often. Silent moments where we'd missed each other. For the most part, he missed me. I was doing my best to be an open book. And still, he came up empty.

But somehow this psychologist had read my mind. And he'd confidently acted on it.

"What makes you think I'd ever be interested in writing a novel?"

"I don't know. But I really like the "For Dummies" collection. I was in the aisle. I saw the book. And for some reason, I thought of you."

"Well, thank you." I didn't tell Greg about the fleeting thoughts I'd had of writing a novel. I was scared that he was beginning to know me better than I knew myself. That morning, I'd carefully looked at my nose in the mirror, and I agreed with him. My nose did fit my face.

The book didn't help the awkwardness between Greg and me. There were long moments of silence that night. It wasn't as easy as it was with Tayo. Not even as comfortable as it was with Malcolm. But the way that he looked at me, I was drawn to that. He really took notice.

"What's that little mark on your face? In between your lip and your nose?" he asked. There was a little pothole there. It looked like the remnants of a mole. In my teenage years, when I didn't receive the acne that adolescents everywhere complained of, I took comfort in my little blemish. Yep, it took a blemish to give me confidence in my crystal clear skin. I thought it added character to my face. Now, of course, I hated the idea of a pimple and I cursed them when they came. But, I had a history with that little pothole, so I didn't mind it.

"I don't know. It's always been there."

"It looks like a scar from the chickenpox. Did you have them as a child?" He touched my pothole. I nodded.

"But I'm pretty sure it's always been there." I wasn't sure, but I didn't like the idea of him figuring out the unknown history of my blemish. He was intruding into my life, my thoughts, my face.

"I'm pretty sure it's from the chickenpox," he concluded.

"Why'd you ask then?" I asked, but I knew why. When you really liked someone, there was no small detail that you didn't mind missing. His interests became your interests. You craved the taste of his culture. You wanted to know his response to every question, even the simplest questions. Like, what do you want for dinner? Or, who's better – Sade or Anita? And you're intrigued by his answer, no matter how shallow or senseless. At least that's how it worked for me.

He didn't answer. Instead, he told me that I should cook for him one day. He'd smacked me straight into the 1950s with that one.

"Why *should* I cook for you?" It wasn't unlike Greg to buy me dinner. We had been out as friends before, and he always picked up the check. But I believed that cooking dinner was an extension of sensuality. It was the reason why I had to get better at it before I got married. A banging dinner, no pun intended, was a form of foreplay even if you didn't eat it off of each other.

"Why not?" he asked, and I found myself considering it. I'd never really made dinner for anyone other than my little brother, and that generally consisted of a cheese omelet for breakfast or meatless spaghetti for dinner.

"Well, what do you like to eat?"

"Anything without tomatoes or onions." I reluctantly threw out the spaghetti idea.

"Is this what you do?" I asked. "Buy girls books and ask them for dinner?"

"No." He shook his head. "Normally, I don't."

And then he kissed me. Again. His lips were just as great as they were the first time. But there was one thing that I didn't like about Greg, aside from how antisocial he was. He never wore shoes. He wore slide-ons with socks every day. I mean, what did he have against shoes? What had they ever done to him? I asked him about it before he left that night.

"What's up with the slide-ons?"

"What do you mean?"

"Why don't you wear shoes like regular people?" I asked jokingly.

"I do wear shoes," he shrugged.

"I've never seen you in shoes with laces."

"I have them though. A closet full. But I wear what's comfortable."

"You should let me give you a makeover."

"I'm not your Ken doll. I would never let you give me a makeover."

"I just think that you'd look great in regular clothes. And shoes." In addition to his slide-ons, Greg wore a t-shirt and jeans every day. No alternatives unless he was going to work. Then he wore a horribly outdated shirt and tie combination. We weren't even together and I was already trying to change him.

Kelvin called me not too long after Greg left that night. We'd grown closer since his visit. I asked him about Rosa, and he asked about Tayo, DJ, Tamika and Brianna. I never told him much about my romantic life, but I decided to talk to him about Greg since they'd gotten along so well at the White Party.

"You remember Greg, right?" I asked him.

"Sure. The one from Tennessee?"

"Yeah."

"Cool guy. Smart too."

"You think?"

"Yeah. Why are you asking? Wait, I know what this is about."

"You do?"

"Yeah. He likes you. He just told you or something?"

"Well, not exactly. But how do you know that he likes me?"

"I'm a guy, Helter Kelter. I guess it was just the way that he looked at you. And maybe the way that he talked about you."

"You could've told me. You should've told me."

"For what? I didn't want to mess up his game."

"So what do you think I should do?"

"What do you want to do?"

"I don't know. He gave me a book, a book about writing a novel. It was a nice gesture but weird. And then, he asked me to cook for him. You know my cooking, Kelvin. I almost killed you back home a time or two."

"Do it. Make him dinner. Why not?" Somewhere along the way, he'd become the mature brother and I the sister in need of advice. I trusted his judgment. I knew that his observations of Greg were probably much better than mine. He hadn't even mentioned his poor taste in clothes. So the decision was made. I decided I would cook for Greg.

The next night Greg played his guitar for me – "Here Comes

the Sun" by the Beatles. I faced him on my bed as he sat on my desk chair, playing. I had no problem watching him play for hours on end. I'd met him four years ago, but I was just getting to know him. Who knew when he'd figured me out, but he'd been much quicker about it.

"One more time," I pleaded. And he started the song again. He even sang along. He wasn't a great singer and he knew it. The sound that came from him was more like a low murmur. It was more than a hum but much less than a belt.

At that moment, I realized that I'd walked right into romantic quick sand. I was pulled under much too swiftly and nauseous because of it. I didn't know what to do with myself.

At the close of the week, Danielle and I went to pick up our cap and gowns from the campus bookstore. We decided that we'd leave Davis just as we came – together.

"Are you guys dating?" she asked.
"I don't know."
"Do you want to date him?"
"I don't know."
"Do you like him?"
"I don't know."
"But, you've decided to cook for him?"
"Yes."
"Why?"
"I don't know."

"This isn't a multiple choice test, Kelly. There are no wrong answers here." That was easy for Danielle to say. She'd been with the same guy for three years now.

"Ok. Kelvin helped me decide to cook for him."
"Your brother?"
"Yeah."
"What did he say?"
"He said that he knew that Greg liked me."
"Oh. Of course," she nodded.
"What do you mean 'of course?'" I asked.
"Well, it's obvious."
"No one said anything to me," I almost yelled.
"I'm sorry, honey. I thought you knew," she lied. I'm sure she knew that I didn't know. I just didn't understand why everyone felt the need to keep it a secret. It occurred to me then that they might think that I would ruin it.

As we waited in line to purchase our shiny red robes, I noticed a familiar cover. *Black Skin, White Masks.* I didn't have very much time left. Maybe Frantz Fanon was the man I'd been trying to meet all along. I sure hoped that wasn't the case. I preferred my men alive and in the flesh.

After we left the bookstore, I finally picked up my copy of *Black Skin, White Masks.* I settled in nice and cozy on my bed with a glass of pink lemonade and a pack of Twizzlers as I began to read.

Loud shouting from a familiar voice outside of my window interrupted me. I opened the blinds to see Brianna yelling at Kenny.

"Are you crazy? Have you completely lost your mind?" she shouted.

Even with my head halfway out of the window, I couldn't hear his response.

"Don't you watch BET? Wrap it up!" she continued.

I grew very curious with that one. Had Kenny gotten someone pregnant? Had Kenny gotten her pregnant? I doubted she would be screaming about it in front of The Villas for everyone to hear if she were the one pregnant. It had to be some other girl. I thought about going downstairs to try to calm her, but it wasn't long before Kenny had his back to her.

"Great. Walk away. You should've walked away a long time ago. Hope you find a bed somewhere." The bed comment caught his attention. He turned around and started toward her.

I still couldn't hear a word he was saying, but whatever he'd said had shut her up. She'd gone perfectly still as he rummaged through his backpack. He found whatever it was that he was looking for and handed it to her. After she took it, he walked away. This time, she didn't shout after him. If I knew my friend Brianna, something wasn't right.

"Coming down, Bri," I yelled out of the window. She looked up at me with watery eyes. Like any friend to the rescue, I threw down my Twizzlers and ran to console her.

She hadn't moved much when I reached her. She was even still staring at my window.

"Bri, what's going on?" I led her to the bench that was a few yards away. She sat down before she began speaking.

"He just," she began to sob. Because she knew she couldn't finish the sentence, she just handed me the box. My only guess was that it was what Kenny had rummaged through his backpack to give her. I opened it.

"Wow. Brianna, is this an engagement ring?"

"Was an engagement ring." she clarified. "He sold his bed to make the last payment." She broke down again.

"Shouldn't you be crying tears of joy?" I asked dumbfounded. "You love Kenny."

"Not now that he got some other girl pregnant," she screamed. I looked around, hoping that no listening ears heard that.

"Are you sure? That she, whoever *she* is, is pregnant? That the baby is his?" I lowered my voice, thinking maybe she'd follow suit. She didn't.

"I know. I know because he didn't deny it."

I considered the questions I'd just asked her. I considered their relevance, and I decided to offer more than the words of a hopeful friend. I decided to just be real. "You've always been too good for him, Bri." She nodded and rested her head on my shoulder.

We just sat there until she had the strength to walk back to her dorm. I walked with her, carrying the little box that she wouldn't, or maybe she just couldn't.

After my talk with Bri, I did get back to *Black Skin, White Masks* that night. Determined to finish it, I studied that book for three whole days, even while taking the last of my finals. It was much too intense to just read. After I finished it, I felt like I'd run a marathon. I wasn't so sure I enjoyed it, but I definitely felt accomplished. I understood why my favorite professor had recommended it.

I didn't have much to do after reading the book. But with graduation upon me, I grew increasingly antsy. Even without a job or a steady man, I was ready to get out of there. I loved Davis, but four years was enough. Three would be too few and five were certainly too many. All of my friends spent their last days in a haste to make more memories. I found myself wishing them by, and annoyed with my mother for her constant nagging about my graduation invitations and party plans.

Planning my date with Greg was like a getaway. I wasn't sure I was cooking for the right reasons at all, but I needed this.

CHAPTER FOURTEEN: MY FAVORITE PROFESSOR

***Self love. It wasn't the name of his class,
but somehow it was the message.***

I hated the grocery store. It was one of the reasons why I didn't cook. I could never find anything. Call me a fool, but everything seemed out of place. I was completely annoyed after realizing that breadcrumbs were not in the same aisle as the bread. Maybe if I cooked more, I'd understand the layout. I guess it was one of those catch-22s.

I found myself pacing the same aisle. Up and down. Up and down. The sour cream had to be somewhere around here. Cold extraneous items like sour cream and eggs should be near each other, right?

"What are you looking for?" asked an older, grey haired woman. "You look the way my daughter looks when we split up the shopping list. Let me help you."

"Thanks. I don't grocery shop very often. My recipe calls for sour cream."

"Oh, sweetie, you're in the wrong section. It's by the cheese, over here." I followed her slow stroll. "He must be very special."

"I'm sorry?"

"My daughter's gotten better with her half of the shopping list since she started dating her new beau. If things go well with you and your friend, I'm sure you'll get better at it too." Her smile was warm and motherly.

"Thanks. I hope he likes it."

"He'll like that you tried."

"I don't know. My cooking could probably run a man away."

"And it's ok if it does. Know what I tell my daughter? It's your relationships, plural, that define you, and your experiences that mold you so long as you let them. Learn from them. Good luck."

That evening I had to call Tamika to help me turn on the stove. It was not as bad as it sounded. Growing up, we had an electric stove, and I still hadn't grown accustomed to lighting my dorm's gas stove. She left once we got it started. Her absence made me a little nervous, but I became hopeful when a pleasant aroma began wafting from the pot.

Remembering the way my mother cooked to music, I put that Drake and Rihanna song "Take Care" on repeat as I chopped, mashed and stirred. Females seemingly had a nurturing nature that went to waste when there was no one to cook for. Even those of us who really didn't like to cook still didn't mind hearing, "Baby, what's for dinner?" For once, cooking felt good.

When he walked in, he just looked around as if he needed to digest the situation before the food. He'd worn his usual get up, jeans and a t-shirt. Slide-ons for shoes. I still had on my cherry printed apron. It was the first time I'd worn it since I'd dressed as a Stepford wife for Halloween. I took it off before we sat down to eat.

Seeing that I didn't have a dinner table in my dorm room, we ate our rosemary chicken and garlic mashed potatoes on my bed. The chicken was a bit too salty. I knew it, but I appreciated him not mentioning it. When I asked him how it was, he just said, "It's good. Good job." And I was happy to see that his plate was clean when I cleared it.

"So what have you been up to now that classes and finals are over?" he asked after I came back with the two cupcakes I'd purchased for dessert.

"I've been reading." I pointed to the copy of *Black Skin, White Masks* that sat on my desk.

"You finally read it. Did you like it?"

"I don't know. I guess it just made me think." It made me think just like my professor had. It made me think just like Greg was making me think now. It didn't take much for me to see the parallels between my obsession with my professor and my newfound interest in Greg.

"I think Fanon reminds us that the issue with race relations isn't one-sided. It's deeper than most of us would like to explore." It sounded like something my favorite professor would say.

"I thought the same thing." We locked eyes at that moment. I was the first to look away, not surprisingly. "Want to watch a movie?"

We watched some mildly interesting movie that night. The title was now irrelevant. The movie was irrelevant. What really mattered was that we grew comfortable with each other. We were finally getting over that awkward hurdle.

He sat up straight while I rested my head on his shoulder. It had taken us four years to explore whatever it was that was there before us. And because of that, whatever it was had grown thick and unavoidable. Intelligently, neither of us made any attempt to duck or dodge it. Instead, we silently watched the movie.

The next day was the day before graduation. My family trickled in from sun up to sun down. But that night, I was excited to leave them to attend Davis' annual graduation party. The event was even bigger than the White Party, and the twenty-dollar entrance fee felt like a bargain. It would be our last hurrah.

Tamika, Brianna and I had carefully chosen our outfits. Brianna had almost thrown out her green sequined mini after her fight with Kenny. Luckily, Tamika had convinced her that there was no point in throwing out such a hot piece of clothing. She'd also made her promise not to bail on us. We were celebrating with each other. Not with Kenny, George or Greg.

The club had four floors, each with its own personality. We arrived before the floors were sticky and the partiers sweaty. We were early, but we didn't care. We partied from the moment we stepped into that warehouse until the wee hours of the morning when we stumbled out. There could've been tears. Maybe there should've been tears because there wouldn't be another undergraduate party for us. That was it. But there was no moment, not even a second, for tears. Just dancing, smiles, laughter, joy, hugs and kisses.

But like that, it was over. We poured into our rooms like little toy soldiers, not knowing what or who we'd meet in the future. Just knowing that we'd be headed somewhere in the morning.

What was it about change that made our stomachs knot? Maybe it was our uncertainty of the future. Would things ever be this good again? Would I ever love this much? Leaving Davis put my stomach in knots, but I didn't have a choice. Change was happening.

To some, graduation day was just warm and sticky. To others, it was the end of a long four, five, six or even sadly seven-year haul. Some were happy, and some were solemn. But most of us were asleep. We were hung over from the party the night before.

I scrambled to get ready on time that morning. With the white dress that I'd carefully picked out for the event, I looked great. I met Tamika in front of The Villas and we walked together to the courtyard for the ceremony.

I remembered the walk well. It was hurried because we were late. But we were among many that shuffled in with shades on to block the sun and hide puffy eyes.

We ran into Greg.

"Late night?" he asked.

"Is it that obvious?"

"No, I saw you two on your way in. I was dropping off a friend. He dialed me at three o'clock in the morning and asked me to pick him up from the party." It didn't surprise me that Greg had skipped the graduation festivities.

"You're a good friend," I said as I stopped to fix his disheveled tie. It was, of course, that same horrible shirt and tie combination I mentioned. But it wasn't so bad that Saturday. Maybe it was the open graduation gown on top, or maybe I was just starting to accept his style.

"I got into Davis for grad school."

"Wow, Greg. That's great. I'll be around. I've decided to stay in Doberville."

He just smiled.

"Kelly. Time crunch," Tamika stressed.

"Right." We picked up the pace, walking in the opposite direction of Greg and hopping into line with our peers in the communications department.

I fell asleep on Tamika's shoulder during part of the ceremony so I could honestly say that our keynote speaker didn't move me. But I did remember seeing my favorite professor. He wasn't on the stage for long, just long enough to give his annual words of wisdom to the graduating class.

He was short and to the point when he said, "This isn't the starting line because it's not a race." Anything he said would've moved me. He could've told us all to eat squirrel for the rest of our lives. He had that powerful pitch to his voice. So it was a good thing his message was indescribably important. Even in the moment, I could foresee that one day I would think back and appreciate those words. It was like that with pretty much everything he'd said. I'd miss his class just as much as I'd miss the cafeteria on Soul Food Fridays, Lemon and Salt happy hours and Davis in the spring.

Throwing the cap had to be the best part of graduation. It was the nonverbal way of shouting, "I'm free." And at that moment, there was nothing better than that and hugging all of my peers right after.

As I searched through the crowd for my family after the ceremony, I bumped into Tayo. I let him embrace me.

"What are you doing here?" I asked.

"I came to see some friends graduate," he grinned. "Congratulations."

"Thanks, Tay."

"I hear you're sticking around." He raised his eyebrows.

I'd saved up enough money for a couple of month's rent from my internship, and I was confident in my ability to find work here. Maybe I hadn't found any other love than this city. And I wasn't ready to give it up.

"Yep. I'm getting my very own apartment. A girl's gotta grow up sometime."

"That's good to—"

He was interrupted by my dad's jeers. I turned around to see my oversized, overly eager family approaching. In addition to my immediate family, uncles, aunts, cousins, grandparents and friends had also shown up for the occasion. The herd of Browns almost trampled me. And then they pulled and pushed me around for pictures. Tayo had disappeared as quickly as they'd come.

We went straight from the courtyard to my aunt's house for dinner. She lived in the suburbs of northern Maryland. They roasted me, a Brown tradition instituted years ago to poke fun of the graduate. They took the jokes back as far as my toddler years so it was late by the time I got back to my dorm. I insisted on sleeping there my last night.

As I packed my last few boxes alone, I ran across the book Greg had given me not even a month before. And I guess something overcame me. Because like I settled in with a glass of lemonade and a pack of Twizzlers to read *Black Skin, White Masks*, I started my first novel. I started it with the Frantz Fanon quote, "In the world I am heading for, I am endlessly creating myself." It was the perfect beginning.

The next morning's sunlight poured through my window. I

had to be up and out of the dorm by noon. I didn't rush getting ready and I welcomed Tamika when she stopped by. She had some of my clothes in hand. As she stepped in, I noticed a small envelope that I assumed someone had slid under my door the night before.

"Wow. You're all ready to go," she looked around my bare room. "You know me, my room is still in shambles." I picked up the envelope.

"You should recruit some helpers. That's what family is for," I said.

"Yeah," she sighed. "Is it really over?"

I nodded.

"What's that?" she pointed to the letter I'd taken out of the envelope.

"I think someone is proposing to me," I said and let my jaw drop.

Tamika screamed. I rolled my eyes.

"I can't believe you fell for that," I said.

"Well, what does it say?" she asked with attitude.

"Let's see." I read it aloud. "Glad you're staying. Your leaving might break my heart. See you around the city."

"Hmm. That's from Tayo?"

"It's unsigned. But I was thinking that it might be from Greg."

"Handwriting?"

"I can't tell."

"Well, just ask them," she offered.

"Maybe I will." I shrugged.

"I should get back to my room," Tamika exclaimed, suddenly teary eyed. "I can't say goodbye to you. So, here are your clothes. Keep mine for now." She waved and quickly left.

I stood in my empty room alone, and I cried incessant tears. I knew Tamika and I would remain friends. I never doubted that. But I also didn't doubt that it would never be the same. Tamika was moving back home to Hartford, Connecticut. We'd been through it all together. And I'd miss her in my memories to come.

She and I met during freshman orientation outside of one of the dorms that neither of us lived in. I was waiting on a friend, and she had been stopped by a guy trying to get her number. I had encountered the same guy earlier that day, and apparently he remembered me.

"Kelly!" he exclaimed when he saw me. He was one of those annoying guys who hit on any girl in his path.

"Hey, I didn't see you there." I lied.

"Do you know my good friend Tamika?" he asked.

Before I could shake my head, she'd responded for me. "Kelly, I didn't even see you there. We should really get going. We're going to be late." She turned to him and repeated, "We're going to be late."

"Don't lose my number," he said, then left us with a wink. Not shortly after, Tamika burst out laughing.

"I thought he'd never leave. Thanks for the out, girl." We got to talking from there and the rest was history. Knowing that she wouldn't be there to interrogate my new dates and I wouldn't be there to call her mid-first date to make sure she was surviving was a sad realization. If things remained on the up and up with George, however, she might not need me to make any calls anyway.

It was over and he, whoever *he* was, hadn't sealed the deal. There was no engagement ring. There was no promise ring. Hell, there wasn't even a man. But as I looked at my naked hand, I realized that it would be holding something just as valuable as soon as I picked up my diploma.

Kanye West once poked fun that a degree would never keep a virgin satisfied. I loved that album of his, *College Dropout*, but he'd missed the fact that college helped so many of us define love outside of the stereotype. I found myself and a new understanding of love at Davis, and that made it well worth the loans I'd accumulated.

Unlike Tamika, I couldn't tell if I'd found the one. But I liked the woman I was becoming and I couldn't hate any of the men who helped me get here.

In the words of the mother who helped me find the sour cream, "It's your relationships, plural, that define you, and your experiences that mold you so long as you let them." But in true Kelly Brown fashion, I kept my fingers crossed for the one.

Love is incalculable, broken in, and unconditional sincere affection. It has no bounds, no size, no body. It is whatever you expect of it on any given day. It gets better with age. It accumulates the little things. It is quietly powerful. And it starts with self.

ACKNOWLEDGMENTS

Most importantly, thank you God for allowing this story to enter my life and giving me the gusto to transcribe it for each of you.

A special thank you to my biggest fan, the first person to love this book, even before I began writing it – my mother, Selena Williams. Your strength and beauty never ceases to amaze me. And to my sister who has adopted so much of my mother's grace, Jaclynn Williams – you are my soul mate and my support system.

A loud and obnoxious shout out to all of my favorite girlfriends. Aminata, Ariana, Ashley S, Breann, Brittany C (your strength eludes me), Candace (a second sister), Daneila, Eboni, Ivy, Kara, Kelauni, Lauren Rivers (full name for you), Nancy, Olamide, Paige, Samantha E, Shivonne, Tiya, Tracey, and Xiomara. Your story is my story and my story is yours.

Thank you to my family. The Williamses, Davises, Barclays, and Wilbourns. A special thank you to the cousins I grew up with – the Moultries. Your faith provided me the backbone for mine. Though I am slightly taller than most of you, I often find myself looking up. An additional thank you to the aunts who have inspired me through their love for literature and writing – Aunt Lavern, Aunt Regina, and Aunt Carolyn.

Thank you to my publisher, Jasmin Hudson, for her insightfulness and attention to detail. And to my second editor, Linsey Isaacs – every writer needs a writer friend. Thank you for being mine. Thank you Francesca Fontenot for your marketing expertise. You are the perfect makings of a best friend. An additional thank you to Steven Jackson for his patience in creating an amazing cover. And to Chris Barclay and Zora Barclay for my lovely photo.

Thank you Dominic, Deonte K, Samantha E and everyone who participated in making this book's trailer.

A very necessary thank you to the many men I have encountered. I love each and every one of you.

Photograph taken by Christopher Barclay

ABOUT THE AUTHOR

JANELLE M WILLIAMS holds a journalism/advertising degree from Howard University. She is the marketing coordinator for Pen & Pad Publishing LLC.

Great writing, dynamic characters, timeless music, entrepreneurial friends, forward fashion, and sweet and salty food inspire her. You can identify her writing by its mirror to reality. Janelle currently lives in Washington, D.C., where she is at work on her second novel.

Contact Janelle at:
Janelleonrecord@gmail.com
http://www.twitter.com/JanelleOnRecord
http://www.facebook.com/JanelleOnRecord
http://janelleonrecord.blogspot.com

CPSIA information can be obtained at www.ICGtesting.com
Printed in the USA
LVOW08s1203150913

352501LV00003B/162/P